I0623702

WRAPPING UP CHRISTMAS

MOVING ON TO A NEW YEAR

A DICKENS HOLIDAY ROMANCE

GRACIE GUY

SUMMER'S GIFT PUBLISHING

Copyright © 2024 by Gracie Guy

All rights reserved.

Print 978-1-956587-22-7

This is a work of fiction. The characters have spent years living in the author's head, until she pushed the freeloaders out and onto the printed page. They are the product of the author's imagination and bear no resemblance to any actual person, living or dead. The names of cities and towns are factual in some instances, but none of the addresses, or any occurrences in this story, are. Any similarities to reality are purely coincidental.

No part of this book may be reproduced in any form or by any electronic or mechanical means, including information storage and retrieval systems, or for training artificial intelligence without written permission from the author, except for the use of brief quotations in a book review.

To GMR Sr. – always!

*To Jean – your beautiful, artistic, non-judgmental heart
has always been a prized gift for me.*

CHAPTER ONE

When her last student left for the summer, Anna started the annual cleaning of her desk—shredding unnecessary papers, packing little tchotchkes from her students, and a quick bleaching of most of the surfaces in her classroom. No, she didn't have to do it; the custodial staff would give it a formal sanitizing before the next school year started, but Anna liked the tidiness she felt in her soul from the mind-numbing task.

And, honestly, she hoped the process would help her shake the "lost" sensation she had felt throughout her twenty-fifth year of teaching. For the first time since college, Anna had no sense of connection with her students, coworkers, or the parents. A sensation that scared her to death.

Eighteen months earlier...

"*You're leaving? When?*"

"*At the end of the school year. Sebastian will be done with his degree and starting a new job in September. He wants us to have the summer to play.*" Her longtime friend absolutely glowed with happiness.

"*But April already left and now you're abandoning me?*" Anna knew she was pouting when she should be happy for her friend, Jeanette.

"*So, April retired as planned and was going to regardless of what happened that summer we were all in Myrtle Beach. She's happy, Anna.*" As the tears started to pool in Jeanette's eyes, Anna felt like an ogre. "*And I'm my happiest when I'm with Seba.*"

"*What can I do for you?*"

"*Just be happy for me. For us. I'm not abandoning you, just starting a new chapter in my life.*" Jeanette hugged her and walked out of the classroom Anna had taught in for over twenty-three years, with her friends on either side.

She let out a deep, sad, sigh. "*Now what do I do?*"

July, Current Year...

A week after the school year ended, during her long-awaited visit from April Stoneman, her older friend had accurately identified what was wrong. Anna was in mourning for her friends. For the daily teasing and overall jocularity they shared—especially at work. When April and Jeanette left the language arts wing of Albany

High School to pursue their happy places, the younger teachers hired were no replacement for the friendship the three women had shared.

Once she'd wrestled with that idea for a few days, Anna decided a change of scenery was the only way to combat her overall malaise. With no specific destination in mind, nor any reservations, she threw a small suitcase filled with casual clothes into the backseat of her Sunburst, along with a cooler brimming with bottled water, cheese sticks, and sliced sandwich meat, and headed east on Interstate-90.

Bopping to a variety of music from the 80s and 90s, screaming along with the lyrics she knew, and making up the ones she didn't, she took in the beautiful summer view along the road that split the state of Massachusetts seemingly in half. After three long hours, she pulled into a rest area to stretch her legs, use the facilities, and find something to eat other than the protein-packed stuff she'd brought from home.

Parking her car at the first available EV station, Anna plugged in the Sunburst, walking away with a smile on her face and a slight jauntiness in her step. The weather was beautiful, and she was on an escapade. Albeit not an international one, but still something new and different. Crossing the clean interior of the venue, Anna grabbed a few of the free magazines and maps stationed by the door, a habit she had developed years before. Every now and then, she discovered a gem of a deal, or an interesting place to visit by scanning the literature. Balancing a Southwestern Rice and Grain Bowl from D'Angelo Subs at the Charlton Service Plaza, she snagged a two-person table in the shade.

Ignoring the people cruising past her on their way in and out of the rest area, Anna unfolded the cartoonish map, triggering childhood memories of traveling with her family. Even though her mom always kept a huge wire-bound copy of the Rand McNalley atlas of the United States in the car, her dad picked up one of these local creations when he found one. As a girl, she loved the tiny hand-drawn sketches of businesses and roads in a township. She'd thought creating the artwork was the perfect job to have. As an adult, she knew these were computer created, but they still spoke to her.

Wrapped in the warmth of childhood memories, Anna spent a few minutes with the friendly snapshot of businesses and things to see and do in Massachusetts, placing her lunch to the western end of the state. Within two spoonsful of savory corn, grilled chicken, and rice, her eyes focused on the word DICKENS. *Hhmm, a Christmas store?*

With no further information available on the hardcopy map, Anna pulled out her cell phone and typed Dickens, Massachusetts into a search engine. In seconds, the screen of her phone began flickering as row upon row of data continued to load.

"Whoa." She scrolled through what seemed like hundreds of links and thousands of pictures. Interestingly, they weren't all winter holiday centric. Many of them were people hiking or riding horses, partaking in street festivals and fireworks. By the time she had finished her lunch, Anna was fully committed to visiting the town. Using the directions link, she locked in the address, cleaned up her table, and practically skipped to her car with excitement. She was on a mission.

An hour later, Anna slowed to the posted twenty-five miles per hour and tooled along the main thoroughfare of the quaint town. Reaching the far end, she turned her compact EV around to retrace her steps, eventually parking in front of what seemed to be an independent bookstore named The Library Cat.

Just as she turned the car off, she instinctively checked her battery level. After having a hybrid for many years, she upgraded to a full EV, which was perfect for her urban lifestyle. However, this was her first long-distance, many-hour trip, and she didn't want to make the mistake of not recharging. From her perspective, driving a green-energy vehicle like hers shouldn't be any different than a gas engine. Afterall, with those, you had to be careful to refill the gas tank often enough when you didn't know the area.

Comforted by her own due diligence, Anna grabbed her purse, sunglasses, and fob from the passenger seat and started exploring. With her bare arms enjoying the noon-time sunshine peeking through the heavy canopy of elms, maples, and oaks, her lightweight sandals tapped along the sidewalk. From smiles on the faces of strangers, to the colorful bounty of flowering containers, everything around her exuded happiness.

Before she'd even finished walking the length of the block, she felt light and giddy, returning grins, head nods, and "good day" greetings. Without a doubt, she wanted to fill her soul to the brim with the optimism. Heading back to her car, Anna decided to spend a few days in Dickens.

Sitting in her Sunburst while she searched for a place to stay, a very smooth and gentle peace settled over her, releasing the tension in her neck and shoulders. As her body relaxed, she felt her back and bottom sink deeper in the seat. *How did I not know I needed this getaway?* Anna sat there for a few minutes, eyes closed, a breeze floating in the window, birds chirping all around her. She heard a dog barking, children laughing, and a far-off lawn mower. All the sounds she would hear from her front porch at home, minus the honking horns and screeching tires of countless cars—and at night, the occasional gunshot.

Afraid she would fall asleep while she waited for check-in time at the B and B she had booked, Anna pulled up the list of attractions she found on the Dickens Chamber of Commerce website on her phone. Just as she started to scroll, an ad filled her screen. She quickly clicked the X without reading the text. But the ad came back. This time she grumbled to herself while closing it.

Deeply engrossed in the list of fun things she could participate in as a solo traveler, the third time the totally unsolicited ad popped up, a few epithets drifted out her open window and into the ears of a passing man, who arched his eyebrows clear into his blonde-ish, wheat-colored hairline.

"Oh, sorry. I didn't mean for anyone to hear that. Again, sorry."

The tall, handsome stranger chuckled broadly and continued along the street. When Anna returned to her browsing, she finally read the annoying advertisement filling the screen.

> PLEASE DON'T CLOSE THIS. If you're still read-ing, we're looking for a few special teachers to join the staff at The BarrSoren Academy. We're not just a school. We're an enrichment program with a new way of teaching. If you're interested, text 21345 and someone will be in touch. PS, thanks for not clicking the X! You won't regret it. ☺

And that is how Anna Miller, the youngest of the five Miller children, found herself returning to the adorable town of Dickens two months later with most of her worldly possessions packed in the moving van she followed.

"HEY, JULIAN. IT'S DANE."

"Yes, old friend. your name is on my screen."

Many years before, IT entrepreneur—Julian Thomas —wrote an app that transferred calls on his cell phone to his laptop without the use of Bluetooth or headphones.

Selling that software the day after he graduated from high school had provided the money to pay his way through college and seed the launch of his one-man multi-million-dollar business, and eventually led him to meeting Dane Rutger, the owner of BarrSoren.

Over four years before, Dane had moved his small, but well-established programming company out of mid-town Manhattan and into a northeastern leaf-peeping town. Most cosmopolitans would consider the new location to be a wide spot in the road. Having grown up in semi-rural Connecticut, Julian always shook his head about the other colloquialisms that also applied like "one-horse town," "a small black dot on the map," and "a one-stoplight town."

In the months leading up to the move, and many since, Dane had tried repeatedly to talk Julian into joining him in the sticks—either as a co-owner or high-level manager. Dane didn't even care if he continued with his own company while fulfilling the needs of Barr-Soren. Julian was sure that today's call was another sales pitch. But he would listen.

"What's the biggest reason you won't come to Dickens?"

"Ha! That should be obvious. The education of my eight-year-old daughter." Julian knew that Dane and his wife, Mari, had a three-year-old, but he'd never discussed things like schools and social influences with him.

"She's in a private school now, right?"

"Yes, sir. She is." Julian furrowed his brow, wondering about the questions.

"That's what I thought. And your excuse is one I've heard from numerous other people, especially from the metro New York City and Boston areas. People have a solid, yet uneducated, opinion of what a small public school like ours can offer. And this is hindering Barr-Soren in our hiring of preferred candidates."

"Dane, where are you going with this?" Julian squinted his eyes in question even though his friend couldn't see him.

"I'm about to launch The BarrSoren Academy. A no-cost learning institution for the children of our employees. It will not be a stand-alone replacement for the Dickens school district, but rather, a supplemental series of programs designed to enhance the good work of the local educators. And by the way, despite its size, Dickens Central School is an excellent district that has graduated many successful professionals."

"Are you looking for feedback on your idea?"

"Yes, and no. I have already obtained approval from the education departments of both New York and Massachusetts, so it's a go starting in the fall."

"Why both states?" Julian loved unravelling his friend's thought process.

"It gives me a bigger pool of teaching candidates. Massachusetts has over seventy thousand. But New York brings in another two hundred thousand plus. If the New Yorkers are already tenured, they are less likely to leave to come here. This way I hope to get responses from both states."

"I'm still confused about the connection to New York. How did you pull that off?"

"Ha! A good question, one with an expensive answer. I reopened the office in Manhattan and added a few new jobs there. It's a much smaller footprint than what we had before, but securely anchors us as an employer in New York state. When you're footing the bill for taxes, they tend to be more likely to invite you into the pool."

"That makes sense. How many employees have signed up for it?"

"None yet—I haven't released it to anyone. Other than my wife and her family, you're the only person who knows what's a-brewing."

Julian waited while the booming laughter from his friend filled the air in his office. "And the students—what do they get out of it?"

"That list is too long for right now. But they do get an educational certificate in addition to their diploma. The certificate will be recognized by colleges in Massachusetts and New York for first year gen-ed credits. I think this will be a game changer when hiring new staff at BarrSoren, let alone the academy."

This right here was a perfect example of why he always listened to Dane Rutger before mentally kicking him to the curb. In short, he was a businessman who thought of alternatives to roadblocks, rather than whine about them. Granted, that was a personality trait of many business owners he'd met over the years, but Julian had found that Dane seemed to embrace employee needs and concerns almost equally to those of his business.

"When do I start?" Julian grinned waiting to hear Dane's response, sure his question would blow his friend away.

"Really? You'll come?" Dane's exuberant response turned the speakers on Julian's computer scratchy for a second.

"Let's start with a visit first. Clare has two open weeks at the end of summer, just before the new school year starts. I want to see how she reacts to being in a rural environment before making the final decision. How about the second week of August?"

"I think you two are going to fall in love with Dickens and its people. Call me closer to when you'll be leaving."

Julian clicked the red phone icon in the lower right corner of his screen with a smile on his face. *What have I just agreed to?*

CHAPTER TWO

A week after returning from her adventure in Dickens, Anna called a family meeting with her brothers and father.

"You're just not thinking straight!" She wasn't sure which of her brothers had shouted first because all four practically climbed over the table in her parents' dining room at her. *And since when do they care about where I live?*

"HEY!" She had to bellow over the clamoring of her family. "This is my decision, not yours. Now sit down."

"But Anna. What about your pension?"

"What about it, Andrew?" She looked at her oldest brother—just five years her senior. "Do you think I haven't thought about it? What do you think my IQ is?"

"Now, An. Don't go getting all prick-aly with me. You're leaving without thirty years of service. Sounds like you're throwing it all away rather than using all that special brain power you like to tell us about."

Anna despised Andrew's pronunciation of the word prickly. *And he knew it, thereby intentionally pushing her buttons.* "All right," *she waved her hand around the center of the table to show inclusion.* "I am not giving up my pension. I won't even have a break in service. I will be on a paid educational sabbatical—kind of like a leave of absence for one year. By way of an organization called NASDTEC, there is an Interstate Agreement that allows me to work in a Massachusetts classroom with a temporary license to teach."

"But it's only good for one year?" *Andrew's right eyebrow arched with skepticism.*

"Yes. And that's enough for me. By then I will either be totally in love with Dickens and the people, or I'll move back here." *She stared into her brother's eyes, the skin around them showing the effects of many years outside.* "There's nothing for you guys to worry about. Even though I will physically be in the next state over, nothing will change with my pension or health insurance. And if I stay in Dickens, leaving my New York pension before thirty years of service, my new employer is contractually obligated to make up the difference."

"What? How can that be?"

God bless my brothers—my dependable protectors since the day I was born. But they need to get out of Albany more.

"Anderson, I just said the two states have a reciprocal agreement. That means I can work in both states."

"I'm not gonna get all fussy with you, little sister, but you did not say it that specifically."

"Listen, guys. I'm tired and I have a lot of packing to do. At this point, I am not selling my house, but I will need all of you to drive by or stop in every few days to keep an eye on it until the tenant moves in"

"Tenant?" Anna looked into her father's eyes, knowing that he would be the one she missed the most. Maybe once I'm settled, I can have him come visit every few weeks or so.

"Yeah, Dad. I'm leasing it to a new professor at Rockefeller College."

And her dad was still on her mind as the medium-sized moving van braked to turn into the driveway of her rented home in Dickens. She had signed a six-month lease on the fully furnished saltbox-style house, with an option to extend the lease or buy the house at either point. At the time, Anna liked that the house was within a mile of the school, a perfect way for her to get her daily exercise. And if it got too cold for walking in winter, she'd drive to school each day.

Her original plan was to use the main suite downstairs and leave the guest rooms upstairs for visitors or storage. But the more she thought about her dad, the more she reconsidered her options.

The process started with Anna directing the movers to each room with downstairs boxes. When the first one marked bedroom came in the front door, the idea of her father coming to live in Dickens popped into her mind, again. She pointed to the stairs. "Second door on the right. Thanks." Then she apologized a few times about the number of belongings she had. But in her heart, she knew her dad would be more comfortable with the down-stairs room.

About two hours after the truck had literally backed up to her new home, Anna stood by herself among count-less boxes, feeling overwhelmed. *What have I done?* She felt her stomach grumble while the negative question floated in her head. *Food. I'll feel better after I eat.*

She scrolled through her phone while contemplating what take-out food she wanted for an early dinner. Her fingers were crossed for a delivery service, but she still had the energy left to get it herself if she had to.

"Oh, this sounds yummy." Anna browsed the menu for Morty's Deli when she heard a metallic knocking sound coming from the front of the house. "Be right there," she shouted out, not sure if the person could hear her. Flipping the lock's tumbler, she pulled the heavy wooden door open to find two women about her age standing on the other side of the screen door.

"Hi, Anna. You *are* Anna Miller, right?"

Forgetting she had dyed her hair to a deep, almost ebony-colored brunette late yesterday, she gave the woman an inquisitive head nod.

"Sorry, I was told that you're a blonde. I'm Mari Rutger and this is Veronica Hawthorne." They each held up the bundle they carried. "We come bearing dinner. Vegetarian lasagna with a heaping side of meat sauce, meatballs, and garlic bread."

"Oh, this is such a wonderful surprise. I am so hungry." She pushed the door behind her until it came into contact with one of the moving boxes. "Please, come in. And yes, I am a natural blonde." She patted her head. "It was time for a change. Sorry about the mess."

"Don't be silly. I think we passed your moving van on our way over. Believe me, we've both been down this road." The tall, blondish brunette gave Anna a warm smile. "Kitchen for these?"

"Where are my manners? It's right this way." Anna began weaving through boxes and smaller pieces of furniture as she crossed the room. "I do know right where my coffee pot is. Do you have a moment to visit?"

"Normally we would say no because one of us would be squeezing this visit in between countless other tasks, but today you get our undivided attention." The lissome blonde's laugh was spontaneous, bringing a quick smile to Anna's tired face.

"Great. Make yourselves comfortable while I pull things together here." After two long months of arguing with her brothers and worrying about her father, glee was a welcome change of emotion for her. "Tell me about yourselves. Mari, are you related to my new boss, Dane Rutger?"

"As a matter of fact, I am. We're married. And every now and then, Dane will mention a new employee he thinks I will like. So, when he said today was moving in day for you, I figured that a hot meal would be welcome."

Anna turned back to the coffee makings a moment, trying to ignore the blush heating her cheeks. "Did he tell you about hearing me throwing epithets from my open car window on my first day in Dickens? I was so embarrassed when I walked into the interview to find the same man sitting there."

"Ha. I'm sure it didn't really bother him. Afterall, he hears me around the horses when there aren't any kids around. But no, he didn't say anything."

Anna addressed her other visitor. "How about you, Veronica?"

"Pull-eze call me Roni. Only my elder relatives on Long Island use my full name." She pointed her thumb toward Mari. "Not sure why she went all formal on you at the door. What she didn't tell you is that her given name is Marilyn, but since she was a toddler, everyone has always called her by her nickname." Both women laughed, leaning on the marble-topped island in front of them.

"Okay, good to know. Roni. Mari. Four letters each." Anna finished making the coffee while the two apparent friends chatted. "Roni, how do you know each other?"

Roni gave a barking laugh, quickly covering her mouth as her cheeks pinked up with blush. "Yeah, you'll figure out that I'm not very good with my 'inside voice.' I've got three older brothers. I grew up in a loud family."

"Really? I've got four older brothers." Both women laughed loudly. "Mari, what about you?"

"Boring. Only child." Mari pursed her mouth, crinkling up her nose, enhancing the spray of freckles across her cheeks. "Anna, everyone at BarrSoren is really excited about the new academy and the programs the kids will be able to take."

"So am I!" Clapping her hands, Anna practically

danced where she stood between the sink and island. "I've been teaching various levels of English for a quarter of a century. This job is like a gift."

"Twenty-five years? You don't look old enough to have been teaching that long." Mari's spontaneous backhanded compliment had all of them laughing again.

"Ha. Ha. I'm going to take that as a good thing. I started an unusual form of student teaching during college." Anna slid two mugs of coffee across the marble. "Cream or sugar?"

As both women shook their heads, Anna slipped onto a stool to join them. After blowing across her steaming drink, Roni picked up the conversation again.

"Tell us about yourself, Anna."

An hour, and another round of coffee later, Mari and Roni wove their way back through Anna's belongings to get to the front door when Roni gasped.

"Oh, cripe. I almost forgot. Dessert should be here shortly. You'll just love Jessica."

"How will I know who she is?"

"Don't worry. She's about yay tall," Roni held her hand up to Mari's shoulder. "She's got very distinctive, rosy cheeks, glittering eyes, and a head full of beautiful curly, white hair."

The pair stopped at the bottom of her front steps when Mari looked up. "And she'll smell good. Don't eat too much of the lasagna we brought. You'll want to save room for whatever treat she created."

Waving and still laughing, her new friends walked to

their car, promising to get together again before school started.

"DAD, where did you say we're going?" Clare's expressive brown eyes looked up from the book she'd been reading while Julian drove.

"To the country."

"But we just passed a sign that said Massachusetts. They have fields in Massachusetts?"

Julian smiled at her innocent question, knowing he'd only taken her to Boston and that was by air. Of course, she would think the entire state was all concrete and buildings. Most people feel that way about New York because all they have ever seen is New York City.

"Right now, we're in Connecticut but soon we'll be in Massachusetts. And there's lots of open space in both states. We're going to a place where they grow Christmas trees and ride horses."

"Real trees?" Her jaw dropped in awe. "Wait, real horses?"

"Yes, and yes, my girl. We're going to visit my friend Dane and his family."

"How much longer?" Clare yawned, quickly covering her mouth.

"About two hours. Long enough for you to take a nap,

chicken." Julian's heart filled with warmth when his daughter smiled at him.

"Dad, you know I'm not a real chicken, but I can be *your* chicken." She patted his arm. "I know you said it's a term of endearment. But I'm not a deer, either."

Trying his best not to laugh loudly in response to his daughter's comeback, he pointed to the pillow on her lap. "Try to nap, please."

Within minutes, Clare was sound asleep, her long, dark eyelashes resting on her alabaster skin, her young lips in a natural smile. Julian wished he weren't driving so that he could just gaze at her, his bright, funny, and beautiful girl who looked so much like her mother, Glynnis.

Nearly seven years before, when Clare was an energized toddler getting into every nook and cranny of their mid-town flat, Glynnis had announced to Julian that she was going to London for a few weeks. At first, she claimed a sick family member needed her support, but that turned out to be a lie. Neither Julian, nor Clare, had seen her since. No video calls, no texts, no pictures—or even social media—in over six years. The woman had simply disappeared. And at this point, Julian hoped she never returned, opening old wounds for them both.

He was pleased that he'd chosen to grab a few small breakfast items from their kitchen and leave Manhattan well before the normal business traffic could start. The further they traveled up I-95 and away from the metro New York City area, the lighter the traffic became, allowing him a chance to relax just a little behind the wheel. Changing to I-91in New Haven the route wove through densely populated areas protected by towering sound barriers. Once in Hartford, he switched to Interstate-84 and rapidly left the metro congestion behind.

When Julian was a teenager growing up in the northeastern corner of Connecticut, all he wanted was to live in Manhattan—the city that never sleeps. But as he approached the Nipmuck State Forest on I-84, he wondered why he'd needed to get away as a younger person. Every mile this trip took them further from the hustle and bustle of city life brought him clarity.

Julian wouldn't force Clare to move if she didn't want to. Leaving friends and everything familiar is hard enough as an adult, but for a young girl, it could be crushing. But honestly, he hoped that by week's end she would find a love for all things country so the change would excite her.

CHAPTER THREE

W ith a light wind playing with the hem of her cotton dress, Anna crossed the parking lot at the main offices of BarrSoren. She couldn't help but grin when she'd found the empty parking spot at an EV charging station. On top of that, use of it was free. Double win for a Monday. Hopefully, her luck would continue for her first meeting as an employee.

"Good morning. I'm here to see Mr. Rutger?"

A slight giggle escaped the lips of the young girl at the reception desk before she covered her mouth. "You must be the new teacher." She offered her right hand to Anna over the bi-level counter separating them. "I'm Lena Brown."

Anna couldn't help but respond to the warm welcome projected by the twenty-something woman, whose cinnamon-colored curls bounced happily when she moved her head, revealing bold green highlights in the lower layers. "Yes. Yes, I am. Anna Miller."

"Hi, Anna. There's a slight change in plans for any appointments on Dane's calendar today." The freckled cheeks of the young woman rolled into a smile. "He's on foal watch, so all of his meetings have been relocated to the farm."

"Farm?" Anna felt her brows furrow in question. "Foal? What's that?"

"Yeah. Confusing right? They live about eight miles out of the village on a horse farm called Creekside Riding Academy. I'll give you directions." Lena dropped into her chair and began frantically scribbling several lines, then handed the sheet of paper over. "The actual address is at the bottom. I just gave you those extra highlights in case you needed standout items to look for in case your signal dies."

"Oh, jeez. Ok. I wouldn't have thought of that."

"You'll get used to things around here." Lena reached under the counter while Anna folded the directions to slip in her purse. "Here, this is some info you'll need before you head out to the farm. Don't worry about the time—I'll let him know you arrived here early."

Resisting the urge to go through the papers, Anna smiled at the young receptionist and turned to leave.

"Oh, hey. How was your welcome lasagna?"

The surprise question from Lena stopped Anna in her tracks. She turned around, slowly, suppressing a strong feeling of privacy invasion. "How did you know that?"

"That's simple. We do something special for each of the new employees and lasagna was the plan for this month. But nobody ever knows what kind of goodie Jessica will whip up for dessert."

As the younger woman leaned back in her chair laughing and patting her belly, the instant apprehension that had enveloped Anna disappeared just as quickly, as a warm smile lit up her face. "Everything was delicious, thanks. And the treats were stunningly decadent mini tarts filled with a creamy cheesecake sort of filling—fresh peaches on some and a blueberry compote on the others, and both drizzled with a raspberry chocolate sauce. I wolfed down four of them before I thought of how many calories were in each."

"Ha! Don't worry. Jessica makes things that are magic, and you won't gain a pound." Lena's laughter continued as Anna waved goodbye.

Once she had the address plugged into her phone, Anna took a deep breath and headed out of the parking lot. Leaving the village of Dickens, the area looked much like the rural environs at home, a soothing familiarity that allowed her to relax another notch.

After what seemed like twenty miles of driving without the mapping software giving her directions, Anna pulled over to check the app on her phone. "Oh crap! Now what?" She stared at the two words in the upper right-hand corner of the screen where she expected vertical white bars: NO SERVICE.

As panic flushed through her body, she frantically looked at her surroundings, and then at the hastily scrawled info from Lena. Anna growled internally when she realized she'd become too dependent upon technology instead of cross-referencing the key locations on Lena's note that would have kept her on the right track. "You can be so careless! We're in the sticks. Where cell phone signals get sucked up by trees, rocks, and dirt. And..." She stopped berating herself when movement on the road caught her eye.

"Oooh, look how sweet." For the first time since her childhood, she found herself mere feet away from a fawn, with barely visible rows of white spots on its tawny, reddish-brown coat. Moments later, a taller version stepped from the brush lining the roadside, approaching the baby with a soft bleating sound as she rubbed her offspring's coat with her muzzle. "This is so sweet." Anna felt her cheeks grow warm as tears formed at the most basic of scenes: a mother loving her child.

"Jeezus Miller, what is wrong with you? You wouldn't be this mushy if the damn thing had run in front of you while the car was moving." Even though she'd chastised herself to hide the swell of emotion, Anna knew that her life had been devoid of sweet and gentle moments like the one unfolding in front of her. "This. I need more of this sweetness."

"Anna?"

The unexpected voice startled her. "Oh my god, what are you doing here?" She stared at the supple figure of Mari Rutger as the accomplished equestrienne dismounted from a very tall, gray horse.

"I was taking the old man for a slow ride before any

lessons started. Meet Snowman." Her gloved hand patted the beautifully arched neck of the horse. "What are you doing sitting here? Don't you have a meeting with Dane?"

"I'm lost." She waved her phone helplessly. "And now I don't have a cell phone signal to figure out where I am."

"Lucky for you we came along." A gentle chuckle escaped as a smile crossed the lightly freckled face looking at Anna. "But honestly, you're not lost. You just haven't gone far enough." Mari leaned against Snowman's broad shoulder, pointing in the direction Anna's car faced. But her new friend's explanation halted when the horse draped his head over Mari's shoulder, reaching toward the open window of Anna's car. Before she knew what was happening, long white whiskers tickled her left arm while his huge upper lip flapped on her skin. Seconds later, the sandpaper-like surface of his giant, thick tongue ran the length of her forearm, stopping only when he sneezed, directly at her, leaving globs of chewed grass across the bosom of her seafoam green dress.

"Oh!" Her shocked retort and instantly flailing arms and hands caused the horse to shoot straight backward from the small car, pulling Mari with him, who quickly gained control of the huge animal.

"Hey, hey, old man. She didn't mean to scare you."

As she looked down at her newly speckled dress, Anna heard the other woman soothe her mount.

"But maybe you shouldn't have tickled your nose on her arm. Then you wouldn't have needed to sneeze all over her."

Mari gently stroked the soft end of the gray muzzle while urging him to stand beside her again.

Anna gaped in awe at how quickly her friend subdued the horse without raising her voice. The swift changes she'd just seen in the gentle giant mesmerized Anna.

"Sorry about your dress. I'll have it cleaned for you."

"Oh, stop. It's just a little spittle." Both women laughed loudly when they both stared at the hopeless mess made on the cotton frock. "Besides, our meeting is on a farm. This way I fit in, right?"

"Oh jeez, you're a good sport. Let me know when you're ready to ride. You'll love how smooth this big guy is." After giving the big lug a full-on hug around his neck, Mari turned back to Anna. "About a mile down the road you'll come to rise in the road that'll give you a big sweeping view of the valley. You can't miss the farm from there. And tell my husband that Snowman is responsible for your tardiness. He was a city boy once, also."

Mari was still laughing as she lifted her left leg, sliding her foot into a silver stirrup.

Anna waited until she was fully seated and had gathered the reins and backed across the road before moving the nearly silent car. "Thanks for the directions." Waving her arm out the window, she shouted. "See you around."

Within a few minutes she pulled into the long gravel driveway of Creekside Riding Academy.

"I CANNOT BELIEVE you're holding staff meetings out here." Julian shook his head at Dane as he waved his arm in several directions. "What does your staff think of that?"

"Most of them like it. The work environment at Barr-Soren has always been casual and laid back, but moving the company here has really shifted that attitude up a few notches. You will be amazed when I show you production numbers since the move."

Julian stood at the open overhead door of a massive red barn, wrapped in an incredible earthy scent that he couldn't quite place. With a deep breath, his body relaxed from the long drive as he exhaled.

The heads of both men swiveled when Clare's lively laughter floated across the grass. Holding the hand of Dane's three-year-old, his daughter's other hand feverishly patted the back of two leggy Foxhounds while the dogs did their best to bestow her with big, licking kisses.

"I think Clare has made some friends." Dane's arms folded across his chest, and he wore a short-sleeved, checked shirt and a pair of worn blue jeans. "You just can't beat that breed for being around kids. They've got a mighty bark when some stranger—human or otherwise—enters the property but it truly is the epitome of the old saying 'their bark is worse than their bite,' because these dogs don't bite."

"Well, if they keep it up, Clare's going to be begging me for a dog." Julian raised his right eyebrow at his friend. "And all the blame will land squarely in your lap."

"Ha!" Dane unfolded his arms, stretching while laughing, nodding his head toward a small red car that slowly crunched its way along the driveway. "Looks like my newest employee is here."

Julian kept one eye on his daughter while the other caught a quick glimpse of a well-tanned arm resting on the open window.

Dane crossed the grass from the barn to the side parking area the car had stopped in. Though Julian couldn't hear the conversation, his friend pointed to the rambling farmhouse that sat at the top of a hill nearly a quarter mile away. Moments later the small car left the barnyard and proceeded up the gravel drive while Dane returned to stand by Julian.

"I've got to go up to the house."

"Well, you do if that's where you're conducting a meeting." Julian raised his eyebrows while stating the obvious.

Dane started toward the red side-by-side about six feet away. Sliding one leg across the seat, his weight balanced on his left foot, he turned to Julian. "Hey, come on up for a minute. I'd like you to meet the new teacher."

When Julian canted his head toward the girls, Dane called them. "Girls. Time to fly." Seconds later, the dogs jumped effortlessly into the back of the UTV while both children scrambled to sit next to Dane.

It shocked Julian how quickly Clare had taken to his

friend. He'd never seen her relax in front of a strange male as easily as she did around Dane. *Maybe it was having his daughter to distract her.* Honestly, he didn't know the answer. But hoped it would play a positive part in how Clare would react when he asked her if she would like to move to Dickens. Pushing those thoughts aside, he filled the remaining portion of the bench seat after belting the girls between him and Dane.

Even though Julian thought the vehicle moved at a very sedate pace, Dane's daughter happily waved her arms over her head as they crested the driveway. "So fast, Daddy."

Penelope's fair-skinned cheeks glowed with happiness. "Hang on dogos." She giggled at her own name for the Foxhounds leaning out from either side of the bed.

The toddler's hands landed on the large, padded dashboard in front of them as Dane pulled to a stop. "Whoa, Nellie. We're home."

Each of them laughed along with her infectious mirth, especially Clare. When her giggles subsided, Julian's heart flushed at the sparkles that lingered in her eyes. It had been a long time since he'd seen her so happy. He crossed the fingers on his right hand fervently hoping her glee was a good sign.

While everyone stood outside the three-car garage, Julian turned reflexively at the sound of the driver's door of the small red car opening. Seconds later, candy apple red toes in a stiletto sandal touched the ground, followed by a long, athletic leg.

Intriguing.

Dark brunette hair twinkled in the summer sun; a bouquet of diamonds danced before him every time she moved her head. When she closed the door and looked up, he saw her face. *Wow! None of my teachers looked like this.* A flash of heat shot through him when a smile accompanied her waving hand. The kind of grin where her cheeks rounded, and her eyes sparkled.

He shook his head a moment, closing his eyes to snuff out the weird feelings that overwhelmed him. *Drop it, Thomas. This beauty might be Clare's teacher in a few weeks.*

"Hi, Anna. I'd like you to meet my friend, Julian Thomas."

Julian stepped forward with his right hand extended.

"Hello, Mr. Thomas. It's nice to meet you." She grasped it firmly and looked directly into his eyes. Seconds later she pulled her hand away, leaving him with an electric flush.

"My pleasure, Miss..." Julian paused, expecting one of them to fill in the information.

"Oh, my bad. Miller. Anna's last name is Miller." Dane corrected his breech in etiquette. He turned toward where both girls stood. "And this is Julian's daughter, Clare," he lightly set his hand on her shoulder. "And my daughter Penelope."

"Hi, girls. I'm Ms. Miller."

The teacher squatted lower, putting herself on eye level with his daughter while offering her a handshake. Pride filled his chest when Clare pumped her arm like a champ.

"It's nice to meetcha, ma'am." After shaking the teacher's hand, Clare stepped back to stand by him.

Julian's gaze was rivetted to the woman as she gracefully rose to her full height, the light green dress slid into place just above her knees, the color triggering whimsical memories of time at the ocean. Except for the rather distinct pattern of green splotches on it.

"What about me?" Dane's daughter tapped the front of the woman's thigh to get her attention before holding her arms up. This time the lithe beauty did a half squat, half bend at the waist, providing Julian with impossible-not-to-look-at decolletage.

"My apologies, Miss Penelope. It's so nice to meet you." Once again, Anna offered her hand to a future student.

"I don't like to be tickled." The face of Dane's precocious child turned mutinous as she perched her hands on her hips. "Why is your dress dirty?"

"Penelope!"

Julian glanced down at his daughter to see Clare's hand fly to her mouth as if to suppress a giggle as Dane scooped her new friend into his arms.

"Let's give Miss Miller a chance to get inside to have some of Gramma's wonderful butter cookies before she changes her mind about the job." Julian watched as Dane tussled his daughter's blonde hair and kissed her cheek and then turned to Anna. "Is that a new pattern or did you get sneezed on by a horse?"

"How did you know?" Her eyes flew open.

"Oh, there's so much you have to learn out here in

Dickens." Dane laughed boldly as he opened the porch door, ushering all of them into the inviting kitchen of the large home that reminded Julian a great deal of where he'd grown up.

With a quick look around the well-appointed space, he felt surprising strings of melancholy pulling him deeper into the possibility of returning to life in a small town.

CHAPTER FOUR

A nna resisted the urge to shrink from embarrassment when the boss's daughter mentioned the mess covering her new dress. What she didn't need at this point was to have the top half of her filthy, especially while her feet were totally overdressed. Having the meeting relocated had thrown her off her game, and then she got lost. *Way to go, Miller. How many exceptions do you think you get before you're packing your bags back to Albany?*

"Anna, there's a bathroom over there if you'd like to refresh yourself before we have coffee."

She glanced toward where he pointed. "How did you know what happened?"

"Ha. This former city boy has learned a lot in the past few years. Did you put moisturizer on before coming here?"

She furrowed her brow at his odd, and mildly personal question. "Why do you ask?"

"That spray pattern has Snowman's name written all over it. Plus, I know my wife was going to exercise him this morning. If he tried to 'kiss' your arm and it had lotion on it, he was bound to sneeze. He has the same reaction when it's bug spray or sunblock. He only wants to kiss skin that is au naturel."

His laughter followed her to the lavatory entrance on the other side of the room. As the tiny surface of her heels clicked across the gleaming tile floor, she pushed the discussion from her head and willed herself to move slowly and carefully. If she lost her footing in front of perfect strangers, it would be mortifying.

When she returned to the kitchen, everyone was sitting at the round table. With an older couple now in the midst, the only vacant chair was next to the way-too-sexy-for-her-senses friend, Julian Thomas. Once again, being careful not to unceremoniously land on her bottom, she kept her eyes lowered crossing the tile as multiple chairs shuffled away from the table.

Reaching the empty space, she looked up in time to discover Julian's arm pulling out her seat, the round muscles of his forearm covered in black hair, flexing as his arm turned. *Did he have those muscles outside?* Her eyes traveled his body, only to find the most enticing brown eyes she had seen in years. His curly locks bounced as he tipped his head to her. *Oh, sweet Josephine. Maybe I should sit outside. Or next to that older guy across the table.* Admiring Julian's full lips, liquid heat traveled to her pelvis, reminding her of the phenomenal drought she'd had in her private life.

Doing a quick fictional locking of her brain, Anna slid into the chair after hanging her purse and leather messenger bag on the back of it. This was a new life for her and no way was she muddying any of the waters by hooking up with the first good-looking man she encountered.

"Anna." Her head swiveled toward the sound of Dane's voice. "I'd like you to meet my in-laws, Ruth and Don Jessup."

"It's so nice to meet you. You have a lovely farm."

"Oh, it's not ours anymore." Don shook his head "We built a nice one-story house over on that side of the property and now Mari and Dane own the main hacienda."

"We've kept it in the family with a new generation of riders coming along to represent Creekside Academy." Mrs. Jessup held out a plate to her. "Here, have a few cookies. They're fresh this morning."

With a slight nervous shake in her hands, Anna did her best to remove two cookies from the offered dish with the small pair of tongs, without dropping them on the table. When the receptionist at BarrSoren told her the meeting location was at the farm, she hadn't expected to meet a gang of people. Her stomach gave a small twist of stress when she thought about presenting her ideas in their company. She hoped all of them but Dane would be leaving before she started working on lesson plans for the newly created school with the new boss.

After about twenty minutes of coffee sipping and cookie nibbling, Anna finally worked up the nerve to ask Julian where he was from.

"Originally, or currently?"

He arched his eyebrow in question, triggering a quick flare of her temper at the instant sensation that he was mocking her by splitting hairs. Afterall, he could have said, "I was born in Toledo but now live in Akron." Or some similar blah blah blah. Instead, he had volleyed the question back to her. *Challenge accepted.* She pressed her napkin to her lips before putting a pleasant smile on her face. "Both."

Anna felt a tiny vibration in his left arm as he cleared his throat. "The fast version is Staffordville, Connecticut and New York City."

Suddenly, his daughter burst into the conversation. "We live at 30 Park Place in Tribeca." The eight-year-old beamed with pride.

"Thank you, Clare." Anna observed Julian's face tightening for a moment.

"Sweetie, how many times have I asked you not to give out our address?"

"But Daddy, Miss Miller isn't in the city. She's here in Dickens." The girl's eyes moistened with tears.

"Don't worry, Clare. I won't tell anyone. But your father is right. Sometimes we need to be careful about how much personal information we tell people."

"I know. Sorry, Daddy." Her dark hair slid forward, covering her face as she looked at her hands.

"So you understand," Julian pivoted his body to face Anna directly. "Professional circumstances require that I keep tight security around myself and my daughter."

Anna snapped her head backward, wondering what

sensitive territory she had inadvertently stepped in. Even though she knew the Manhattan address was enviable, nothing about the clothing he wore, or the car parked by the barn, screamed wealth or notoriety.

"Julian and I became friends after we each made our splash into the technology world." Anna looked at Dane as he jumped into the conversation. "He was actually ahead of me on the curve. Now we're just two guys raising daughters and enjoying the fruits of our labors."

"Speaking of work, I do have one report I need to review for a client before nightfall." Julian signaled for his daughter to stand with him. "Dane and Penelope, thank you for the barn tour. Mr. and Mrs. Jessup, thank you for your hospitality." As Clare stepped to his side, Julian extended his hand to Anna. "It's been a pleasure."

Dane rose from the table as the two headed toward the door. "I'll be back in a moment. Just need to run these two down to their car."

"We'll take care of that." Ruth Jessup tapped her husband's shoulder. "We need to get some groceries."

After what seemed like a mass exodus, Anna looked at Dane. "Did I say something wrong?"

ALL RIGHT, *so it wasn't so smooth of me to freeze her out like that.* As he and Clare drove back into the business area of Dickens, Julian had plenty of time to dissect his reaction to Anna Miller's questions. He assumed that she was fully familiar with his friend's wealth, mostly because there had been plenty written about Dane's decision to move his company to the bucolic New England town.

Instinctively, Julian withdrew from the shortsightedness of assuming Anna knew anything about him just because he and Dane were friends. Unlike his gregarious friend, he had taken great pains over the years to keep his name out of the limelight, and away from women who might be looking for what many perceived as a swanky lifestyle. Did he crave a deep and intimate relationship like he thought he'd had with his ex-wife? Yeah. Honestly, he did—despite the outcome of the short-term marriage they had shared.

Also, Julian wasn't comfortable with women fawning over his looks or his wealth. By contrast, he was the protective, single father of a young girl whose biological mother had abandoned them both. In his mind, his most important job was to raise Clare to be a confident woman who never doubted her worth, or her abilities. Unfortunately for the borderline craving he had for Anna Miller, he would not be "hooking up" with anyone, any time soon.

"Dad, are you mad at me?" Clare's big eyes stared at him from across the table he'd chosen at Morty's Deli.

"Honey, why would I be?" He reached past the condiments separating them and covered his daughter's hands with his own.

"It seemed like it back there at the farm."

"Yeah, I'm sorry I reacted so quickly. Do you want to know why?" Julian hoped she would decline the offer but gave up that idea as her head bobbed up and down. Looking around the busy place, he was glad they had chosen a table by the window, giving them at least a modicum of privacy.

"Honey, do you know what it means to be rich?"

Clare shrugged her shoulders and shook her head. "Not really. I guess it means to have lots of money. What's wrong with that?"

"Yeah, pretty much." Julian watched her eyes to gauge her emotions. "Sometimes when you have lots more money than others, bad people try to steal from you."

"You mean like, taking your wallet or watch—like a mugging?" Clare's brown eyes turned wide as she pursed her lips.

"Yeah, that'll work." No way was he scaring her with talk about abductions and ransom. "And maybe expensive things in your home."

"Dad! Like all my dresses and tiaras from when I was little?"

Julian tried not to chuckle at his daughter's question. She had no idea that the glitter and "gemstones" covering her frocks consisted of plastic and paint, but he was pleased that she was still infatuated with them. "Yeah, maybe." Much to his surprise, Clare's mouth formed an O and her eyes grew wider. "But honey, that's not what I'm trying to tell you. And don't worry, I set the alarm before we left."

"Oh. Okay, Dad." She let out a long, dramatic breath for a kid, leaving him to wonder where she'd picked up the habit. "Then what are you saying?"

"Do me a favor and don't tell people what our address in New York is, okay?"

Clare shrugged her shoulders and gave him a questioning smirk as she held her palms up. "Well, duh. Okay. We're not in the city so I thought it was okay. Now can we order lunch?"

Julian had no idea how her mind hopped from innocent girl to testy daughter so easily. But he hoped she wouldn't turn into one of the disrespectful and demanding she-monsters that he'd heard about from some of the parents in his business circle.

Even though they'd dawdled their way through lunch, they still had over an hour before check-in at their chosen temporary residence, Victorian Hall at Pickwick Acres. Dane had recommended it, assuring Julian that the atmosphere would be casual, and that Clare would be in no danger. Dane had even put a call into the owner, Sydney, to see if her own children would be around this week.

Julian replayed the conversation with Dane in his head.

"Hey, stay at Victorian Hall at Pickwick Acres. My friend, Sydney, is the owner. And her kids are done with summer camp, so they'll be around next week. It'll give Clare lots to do while you and I discuss business."

"What? You think I'd leave her with a stranger?"

"Jesus, Thomas. I leave my own daughter to play with

the Smith kids. Believe me, Sydney would never let anything happen to her."

Hearing the edge to his friend's voice, Julian decided he'd been too judgmental. "Okay. I'll book a room there."

"Maybe I can learn how to relax a little around here," he mumbled to himself as he and Clare window shopped along the main street of Dickens.

But that was an internal battle not likely to be resolved easily; one that would take way more than a single week to convince him to loosen his grip on his daughter. Even if no one knew how wealthy he was, there was always the very real and frightening possibility of her mother returning to their lives.

When he heard his daughter giggling a few feet in front of him, Julian looked at the sign over his head. FURRY BOTTOMS PET STOP. *You bloody idiot, get out of your own head and back into the present.*

"Daddy, look!" The grin plastered to her face was almost too much for his curmudgeonly soul. "Puppies!"

Julian did his best to sound enthused. "What have you found there, chicken?"

"Can we go in? It'll only be for a minute. Pulleeze, Daddy?"

Her young head tipped coquettishly, as if to sway him in her direction. Again, he wondered where she picked up these habits.

"Okay." He held his hand up while Clare danced with excitement on the sidewalk. "But two rules. First, we can't stay long because we don't want to be late for our check in. And secondly, we are not getting a dog.

Do you understand me? No dog at the Thomas hacienda."

Clare rolled her eyes and shot past him to the door. As she yanked it open, she turned her head to him. "I know. No dogs in New York." With that pronouncement, she did her best to flounce into the store, giving the door an ineffective slam as the large piston took control, moving it at a snail's pace.

CHAPTER FIVE

"**A**s you know from my resume, my background is in English. There are several other topics I would have liked to dabble in, but there is such a huge need for TESOL in the Albany area that I couldn't squeeze additional courses into my schedule."

There was certainly more to it than that, but Anna didn't see any reason to enlighten her new employer with personal details about her friends leaving and how teaching in Albany had lost its shine.

"Well, now that we're finished with all the required talking points like health insurance and time off, my kitchen is your platform. Speak your mind." Dane chuckled as his arm swept the otherwise empty room.

For the next hour, Anna pulled out lesson plans ranging from the standard tutoring for English to art history and researching the masters, managing a household, and balancing a checkbook, protecting your privacy online, and her personal favorite: photography for social media.

"That's an intriguing topic. Tell me more about it." Dane tapped his finger on the folder.

"As the title suggests, we'll be analyzing the pictures people plaster all over the various social media platforms. But it's not just a fun way to play with phones. It's actually more of a psychology course looking at the material from a variety of angles—what is the poster projecting? What are they hiding? How much is staged? What are the intended subliminal messages?"

"Whoa, can I assume you've designed this for the more mature students, only?" He interrupted her before she could finish her description.

"Of course, sir. And I won't allow any nudity, profanity, or objectification of people—females or males." Anna expected this course might be a heavy lift for the parents of a smaller school district. "My intention is not to promote, nor romanticize, the notion of how the students can sell themselves to others. But rather to have them think objectively and to question themselves about the messages people are sending, if only in a subliminal fashion."

"Let me just tell you up front that you will probably get pushback on this class. While people around here tend to be earthy, if you will, there are many farmers who have supported several generations of families from their land and animals. Production and reproduction are a fact of life. But not a sexualized one."

"And this course isn't, either. We're not looking at

who is sexy. We'll be questioning influencers and–or celebrities, with and without their families. I'd also like to explore the true price these people are paying—having their personal life available with no boundaries—to receive a paycheck. Objectively speaking, I believe they are paying in morals well above what they are acquiring in dollars. I think it's important to have young people recognize the importance of a code of ethics, applying good judgment, and the importance of the moral code their parents have established for them."

Anna tried to hide the slight shake in her hands as she shuffled papers around the table before returning them to the manilla folder. She didn't need to teach this course, but she wanted to. Every year the dresses she'd seen worn to the junior and senior prom were shorter and tighter. She wanted young people to question why the fashion world needed to sexualize them. Anna knew it was complicated, but she felt it was important that young people—especially girls—understood the importance of their mind, not just their looks.

"I suggest you pull the social media class from the offering for at least the first semester."

She felt her stomach drop at the denial, but she wouldn't let her disappointment show.

"You are new to teaching in this district, and new to living in the area. I think you need to spend time getting to know the families, the children, and their abilities—or lack thereof—and the general pace of life around here."

"Yes, sir." Anna cast her eyes to the folder in front of her.

"Anna?"

She looked up at his question.

"There is no need for such formality with me. We're not in the military and I'm not your older male relative. But I *am* someone with your best interests at heart. If you try to insert what many people will think of as interference in their personal family dynamics, there will be a groundswell of calls for your resignation or dismissal."

Willing herself to breathe, Anna wouldn't let her eyes wander from her employer's face.

"There are many good people in Dickens, and you will find that they welcome you with open arms. Let's give both you and all of them a chance to get to know each other before your career is dragged up the steps of a guillotine platform."

"Thank you, Dane. I appreciate the guidance." She rose from her chair, assuming he had ended their meeting.

"I saw the moment your face fell. Don't let this discourage you. I'm not saying the course is without merit —I'm saying that you should not rush into introducing it." Dane's chair scooted across the tile floor as he stood, offering his right hand to her. "You'll be great here. Welcome aboard."

"Thanks. I'm looking forward to a new chapter." She smiled slightly, as he held the kitchen door open.

Anna put the smackdown on her emotions as the small EV crunched its way down the driveway, being sure to wave to Mari as she drove by the barn. Pulling out on the quiet country road, she decided to meander before heading back to BarrSoren to acquaint herself with her new office.

Winding back to town along the blacktop, she drove past trees and crumbling stone walls, lichen and vines hiding much of the surfaces. Anna was surprised by how much detail she had missed on her way to Mari and Dane's farm—something she squarely attributed to nerves and her fear of getting lost.

"You knew this job was a gamble. But what choice did you have?" With her own question hanging in the air, her eyes caught sight of a neglected farmhouse about a hundred yards from the road. When she found a break in the stone wall, Anna pulled in and turned off her car. She sat there a few minutes, squinting at the old paint, much of it faded to a dirty gray. On a gust of air, a shredded curtain flapped through a broken window, stirring up a memory of an old house she found years ago near home.

Deep in thought, Anna got out of the car and took a few steps into long grass in her overdressed heels. She felt the long spike sliding into the soil, probably ruining the cloth that covered them, trying not to contemplate how much money she had just wasted. *What are you doing?* She needed to get closer to the building.

A few yards before reaching the front porch, she found her path blocked by a large, intricate web made by an orb weaver. Looking down at the massive black and yellow spider, its long legs arched to skedaddle across the luminous surface the moment something touched the silken threads. Years before, Anna had learned that this type of spider held venom to kill their smaller prey but was of no threat to her.

Looking around the web, there seemed to be another one in each direction, effectively blocking her from reaching the house. "Crap. How many did I just walk through?" This thought, coupled with the instant realization that she was also in major tick territory, caused a shiver to run down her spine.

"Okay, Ms. City Chick. Apparently, you've forgotten the rules of nature. This abandoned yard is theirs, not yours." She shook her head and lifted her shoulders reflexively, hastily retreating to the safety of her car. Before she climbed in, she shook the light cotton of her dress and glanced at her legs. Finding no dark brown bugs hitchhiking on her, Anna slid into the driver's seat with her eyes rivetted on the neglected building.

"It's got a story. Now I just need to find a person who can tell it to me." With a new project filling her head, Anna returned to the road, smiling. Since her childhood, she'd romanced the history of forgotten farmhouses. As a realistic adult, she expected it would take a pretty penny, but her heart longed to bring this one back to life, to give it a family, to make it a home.

AFTER NEARLY AN HOUR in the pet shop, countless colors of dog hair covered Clare. But she was happy.

Something that had not escaped Julian's notice.

"Hey, kiddo. We've got to go."

Her beautiful doe eyes looked up at him over the head of a puppy. "I know, Daddy. I'm coming." Gently she slid the pup from her arms and back into the pile of pine shavings, stood up, and climbed over the twelve-inch-high enclosure.

Julian turned toward the shop owner, whose watchful eye had never left the litter of pups. "Thank you for letting my daughter play with them. Unfortunately, we're just visiting Dickens for a few days so we're not in the market to take one home."

"Yet."

Julian looked down at his daughter's expectant smile but wouldn't budge on his stance.

The woman standing near them extended her hand. "Thank you for coming in. I'm Linda Abernathy. Just so you know, this is the last litter of puppies that we will be offering at Furry Bottoms. When I took over ownership of the shop from my parents, there were outstanding contracts with a few breeders to which I was obligated. After this, I will be working closely with the Dickens Animal Rescue to find homes for older dogs who still have love to give."

Julian smiled at the information. He knew people had specific reasons for buying a purebred from a reputable source. But he'd also heard enough horror stories about puppy mills to prefer not to support them. If Clare agreed to move to Dickens permanently, he would return to Linda's shop to make a personal connection to the rescue organization. And because he was at heart a total softy, make a generous donation at the same time.

Leaving the store, Julian held the passengers' side door of their older model Jeep for his chatty daughter. From the moment they stepped onto the sidewalk, Clare had kept up a constant stream of information about various dog breeds, which were more suitable for city living, and those breeds that were compatible with the colder weather of living in the north.

Sliding into his own seat, he paused a moment to look at her. "Young lady, where did you learn all of this information?"

"Come on, Dad. The Internet."

He tried not to wince at her simple answer as he thought about the trolls with ill intentions swirling about the amassed data pool. *Stop it. It's just information about dogs.* "You have certainly been researching, haven't you?"

"That's the Girl Scout motto." Clare's head snapped up, throwing her shoulders back and arching her spine. "Be prepared."

"Did your troop leader tell you that?" Julian did his best to keep his tone, and facial expressions, business like. From the moment she'd become a Daisy Scout two years before, Clare had taken the motto and the slogan quite seriously. Though there were some days where "do a good turn daily" had involved rescuing a spider or bug, she still applied a gentle touch.

"Yes. I want to be ready for when you say yes to a puppy."

"Does it have to be a baby? What about an older

dog?" Pulling up to a four-way stop sign, he snuck in a quick glance at her face.

Her brow furrowed. "I could try loving a grown dog. But I really want a puppy."

Their conversation dissected the topic for a few more miles until they reached the Victorian Hall at Pickwick Acres.

"Oh, Daddy. This place is so pretty. Is that a mansion?"

Julian glanced at the rambling white colonial, wondering where the original house stopped, and the additions began. Massive oak and maple trees in the front and side yard shaded the house from the afternoon sun while the upper leaves of the graceful giants danced slowly in a lazy breeze.

"Clare, this is what's called a bed and breakfast. Basically, you pay a fee to have a private room to sleep in and breakfast the next day."

"But you can stay in a hotel to sleep, right?"

"Yes, but there are none available here. Besides, I thought you might enjoy a place with stuff to do outside and other kids around."

Clare tipped her head. "Dad. There are other kids? My age?"

Julian nodded.

"What is there to do?"

He pointed toward the barns and woods beyond the main house, causing his daughter to squeal with delight. "No city park here, kid. We're out in the country this week."

The moment the Jeep came to a stop, Clare popped her seatbelt and slid her long, slender body out of the vehicle, yelling for him. "Come on, Dad! Look at that huge dog!"

Julian's head whipped around to discover something large and hairy loping toward his ecstatic daughter. But before his own fight-or-flight reaction kicked in, causing him to make a bumbling spectacle, a woman came running from the side door, barking orders at the dog.

"Heel, Hank. Don't jump on her. Be gentle." Seconds later, she arrived to grab the thick leather collar of the jocular giant, drool flying through the air, causing more laughter from Clare.

Julian leaned against the hood of his car trying not to add to the confusion.

"Hi. I'm Sydney Smith. Welcome to Victorian Hall at Pickwick Acres."

Julian shook her outstretched hand. "I think you can let go of Hank." He pointed to the other still holding what looked like eighty pounds of hairy happiness. "I'm Julian Thomas and this is my daughter Clare. We have reservations."

The young girl loosened up one arm from hugging her newest friend.

"Of course. You're Dane's friend from New York City. Welcome to Dickens."

"Thanks. We're looking forward to a week of relative peace, quiet, and fresh air." No sooner had he finished his sentence when Sydney's dog bolted from the hug Clare was still giving him, throwing her backward before racing across the lawn, barking feverishly at a chipmunk that tossed taunting chirping sounds from halfway up the massive oak.

When Julian's eyes fell to his daughter, he realized that she was laughing at the lumbering hunter, not crying from injury. Once again, her flexibility in situations never ceased to amaze his stoic personality.

I might need this move more than Clare does. The surprising thought filled his mind as he grabbed their belongings and they both followed Sydney into the inn.

CHAPTER SIX

Over the next three days, Julian saw far less of Clare than he expected. She had fallen into a fast friendship with Sydney's children, along with several others from town. Clare had even spent time at Dane's farm, learning about horses and riding, with his friend's wife. Based upon their nightly dinner conversation, she was having a grand time in the fresh air.

"Clare seems to be having fun." Dane pointed out the triple-pane window of the BarrSoren conference room.

Julian moved to the solid glass, wishing it were open so that he could hear the laughter coming from the playground created for the children of employees. "It's been amazing to listen to her recap each night. It's almost like she's someone else's child."

"How's that?"

Julian felt his friend's eyes on him.

"She likes it here, right?"

"As far as I can tell, she loves it. Listen, this is a kid who hasn't willingly socialized with children her own age. There aren't that many in our building and none of them go to her school. As a result, she's always been a bit reclusive."

Dane started laughing as his finger lightly tapped the tinted glass. "You would have trouble convincing my wife of that. She said Clare was a magpie in the barn. And look at her now—the Pied Piper of the playground."

Julian chuckled as he returned to the leather conference room chair. "There's something about the clean air up here."

Dane's eyebrows went up, but the man didn't interrupt him.

"I'm seriously considering the move."

"Wow, that's great news." Dane slapped his shoulder before sliding into the chair kitty-corner to Julian. "Do I hear a 'but' coming on?"

"Well, first of all, I haven't said anything to Clare. I'm concerned this excitement is short lived because we're visitors. What happens if she's two months into the school year and starts to struggle? Will I have destroyed her life?"

"Not likely. Kids are pretty resilient and the younger they are, the easier the transition. And if it looks like she's troubled, let her spend more time at Creekside. My wife and father-in-law, along with their large assistants, are the best at developing and restoring confidence."

"That's one half of the equation running through my head. The other part is business." Julian took a swallow of water before announcing his proposal to Dane. "I would like to join you in a partnership that is a spinoff of both of our companies."

"Intriguing. What's the premise?"

"At the risk of sounding extremely egotistical, you and I share a staggering wealth of knowledge regarding computer programming. And we both have a knack for staying abreast of current trends in gaming and project management software. But there's an area neither of us has tried."

Dane leaned forward, placing his elbows on the table, apparently waiting for more.

"I say we take on educational programming."

"Whoa, that's a broad topic. I mean, that can cover the obvious of elementary through high school curriculums, collegiate programs, or even employee development in businesses."

"It is, but we only need to take a nibble at it to begin with. This new school you've designed has serious potential for developing extracurricular knowledge that compliments the standard needs and broadens a child's background. Except for tutoring programs, let's leave the traditional three Rs to the old guard. Allowing us to get creative and downright inventive."

"My friend, that's exactly what I had in mind with the Academy. Unfortunately, I couldn't get buy-in from the two state eds without dialing it back to more of a tutoring plan."

"Listen, I haven't fully fleshed this out. But we're both in a position with our businesses to take this plunge.

Fingers crossed that we succeed with it. If we don't, Clare and I still benefit by getting out of the city."

"I love it." Dane stood, offering his hand to Julian. "Let's catch some lunch and do some brainstorming. Any chance you fancy some deli?"

"Sure. Sydney Smith is picking up her kids and Clare to take them back to Victorian Hall for lunch. Lead the way. I'll text her while you drive."

For the next two hours, the friends tossed ideas back and forth over soup and sandwich perfection, eventually returning to the parking lot of BarrSoren. The more ideas they came up with, the more excited Julian became. It moved him to enrich the lives of others through knowledge, regardless of age. With the barrage of topics that popped out of their mouths the whole time, Julian was sure they would have success moving into the area of supplemental educational programming.

"Before I forget to tell you, when I sat down with Anna Miller the other day, she had this really great idea about a class called Photography for Social Media. Basically, it makes kids think about how they are influenced by all of it and how it affects their own morals."

"Sounds interesting, but is she questioning the guidance parents are already giving their children?" The hair on the back of Julian's neck started to stand up. From the moment he'd laid eyes on those stilettos, he wondered what sort of influence she would be on his own daughter.

"Oh, chill Poppa Dog." Dane gave Julian a faux punch in the shoulder. "I already told her that I don't want it in this year's curriculum offerings. She needs to learn about the town and the people of Dickens. But what she proposed is certainly interesting. Maybe we can use her as a SME when we get that far."

"Subject Matter Expert?" Julian pushed himself off the side of his Jeep where he'd been leaning casually in the sunshine. "What makes her an expert in morals?"

"Did something happen between you two? Why are you so quick to question her?"

Julian thought about Dane's question, wondering about his instantaneous response. "No, nothing. I don't even know her. Ignore me."

"Good to hear. Hey, Julian. I've got a meeting with HR in about fifteen minutes. Let's work out the business details tomorrow."

After releasing Dane's hand, Julian yanked open the driver's door and slid into the aging leather seat with two colossal thoughts weighing on his mind: keeping both him and his daughter away from the attractive Ms. Miller and discussing the possibility of a move with Clare.

ADMITTEDLY, it had taken Anna a few days of licking her proverbial wounds after Dane shot down her social media class before she relocated the joy she'd discovered since moving to Dickens. But with decades of teaching experience, she had learned long ago to cover her emotions with Teflon, a character trait she had depended on for years to save her heart from injury, both personally and professionally. In short, she allowed herself two days of huddling under a well-worn family quilt sucking down bon bons and watching chick movies on her couch.

This morning she'd followed her father's advice before heading to work. Take a hot shower, eat a hearty breakfast, and put a smile on your face. She giggled lightly while walking to her office at BarrSoren, thinking about her dad and his favorite catch phrases. As her eyes began to mist, Anna couldn't deny she missed their almost daily visits. With her mother gone over five years, Anna had stepped in as his nurturer despite him being quite capable of taking care of himself.

"Oh, so sorry." Anna instinctively put her hand up, as her eyes flashed from looking down to settle on the warm, chocolate color of Julian's. "It's you." *Oh chick, look away. This guy is so attractive he's dangerous. What you wouldn't do to snuggle up to those peepers every night.*

"Good morning, Ms. Miller. You appear to be a bit distracted. It's a good thing neither of us are driving a vehicle."

For a single millisecond Anna's temper flared in offense at the statement from the devilishly handsome Julian Thomas. But just as quickly, she let it go and sunk to the deep end of the swimming pool that was his velvety brown eyes—so dark they were nearly sable.

"I'm sorry, I was just a little engrossed in my thoughts."

His gaze left hers, floating down to where her hand still pressed against his chest.

"Oh, pardon."

"No problem."

For a quick second, Anna thought she'd heard him suck in his breath as she dropped her hand to her side. "Planning my day. And yes, I was a bit distracted."

"No harm done." Julian semi-turned to look over his shoulder. "Dane had an emergency call, so I thought I'd stretch my legs." Now he pointed to the executive suite. "Early meeting to hammer out some details. You know what they say about them."

Anna burst out laughing. "The devil's in them."

Before she could get her emotions in check, tears filled her eyes over her father. Julian's large hands gently cupped her shoulders, causing the bloody emotional moisture to roll uncontrollably, wreaking havoc with the eyeliner she had applied earlier.

"I'm so sorry." She swiped the back of her hand across each side of her face, sure that she had added more wrinkles to the delicate skin. "Too many thoughts for so early in the day. I have to go now."

Pulling out of his warm grasp, she practically ran down the carpeted hallway, berating herself internally for blubbering. Moments later she slammed the solid door behind her, leaning her back to the cool wooden surface before sliding to sit on the floor.

"What are you, like twelve years old?" She mumbled into her hands cupped over her face, feeling the heat of her embarrassment while catching a whiff of a uniquely male scent. "Sure. Tall, perfect hair, eyes like chocolate pudding, and he smells great."

Anna drew her knees up to her chest, wrapping her limbs in self-comfort.

"This is just lust. Your non-stick emotions have not failed you." She shook her head and slowly slid her way back to a standing position, thanking her hamstrings for staying powerful even though she had neglected exercising of late.

"Anna?"

She jumped away from the door at hearing her name muffled slightly.

"Are you all right?"

Pushing down on the brass lever, Anna pulled the wood inward to find Roni Hawthorne.

"I saw you run past my office and then heard the very distinct slam of a door." The manicured brows of the taller woman seemed to ask her a question.

"Yeah, thanks. Just had a little surprise, that's all." Anna wanted to invite her to visit but was afraid she wouldn't be able to control all the questions tumbling through her head. Like seriously, how much could Roni possibly know about Julian Thomas, anyway? It was absurd but if she made a single inquiry, she worried she would sound like a fourteen-year-old ninth-grader ogling the quarterback of the football team.

"If you're sure, then I'll get back to work."

As Roni turned to leave, Anna caught sight of what looked like a baby bump. With a flashback to the time another teacher had labeled her as pregnant when in fact she had merely overeaten, she kept her thoughts to herself. She was content to wait for Roni to share any private news.

"Oh, hey. Have you got time for lunch? Mari and I plan to meet at Dorrit's Diner."

"If you're sure I'm not interrupting anything."

Roni chuckled before responding. "The two of us talk or text, or sometimes both, almost every day. Believe me, we get plenty of private chat time. I'm sure she'll be glad to see you."

"Then yeah, that would be fun."

The warm smile covering Roni's face as she walked away confirmed Anna's decision. She propped open the door and crossed the office to her desk, gazing out the window before sitting down. *Yes, you miss home. Yes, you miss your dad. And even your brothers. But you made this choice, now make it work.*

She settled into the ergonomic chair that Dane's receptionist, Lena, had ordered as an apology gift for the day Snowman had sneezed all over her new dress. *Ah yes, her unforgettable first day at BarrSoren.*

Opening her laptop, Anna watched as brightly colored images filled the screen of the attached monitor, which was twice the size of her first television. She had to admit there had been advantages to being the only girl in the Miller clan. Her brothers had shared bedrooms and TV sets, while she had her very own of everything.

She scanned a spreadsheet that Lena had emailed to her. She had put many hours into designing the curriculum with oversight from Dane. With the first day of school coming soon, Anna was pleased to see the number of student names already enrolled in a few of the afternoon classes. Maybe Dane was right about the residents of Dickens being ready to embrace her once they got to know her a wee bit. Hopefully by January the enrollment will have grown enough to hire an additional teacher.

CHAPTER SEVEN

"How was your morning, kiddo?" Julian had interrupted his planning meeting with Dane to pick Clare up from Victorian Hall, take her to lunch, and then to Creekside Academy for her afternoon with Mari.

"Daddy, it was so exciting. Ms. Smith took us hiking through the back woods and up a mountain. At first Avery and Ryan thought it was boring, but their mom said they were being spoilsports and were going to ruin it for me." She twisted her mouth, a clear indicator she was thinking. "After that they got laughing and acting fun."

"Did their dad go with you?"

"No. Mr. Archer had to pick up an order from the feed store. He says he's getting ready for winter before the birds are. They eat black oil sunflower seeds." Clare nodded her head to Julian, looking very much like the old farmers he knew as a kid—comfortable in their knowledge and straightforward with what they said.

"It seems like you're having a good vacation."

"I am. But school starts soon." Clare's voice dropped nearly to a whisper as she turned to look out the window. "I don't want to go back to that school."

Julian pulled over in the widest portion of shoulder that he could find on the country road. Pivoting in his seat behind the wheel of the older Jeep, he tapped his daughter's arm. "What's the matter sweetie? Did something happen last year?"

After a minute of silence, Clare let out a deep breath and faced him. "I don't have many friends and it's not fun. Can we live here in Dickens?" Her face sagged with sadness.

"Why didn't you tell me this before now? I thought you liked it there."

"That's 'cause I didn't have friends like Avery and Ryan. And they have lots more friends that are our age. Please, Dad?"

Overwhelming disbelief washed over Julian. The topic he was worried about broaching just got dropped into his lap by an eight-year-old.

"Are you sure about this? School starts soon which means we'd have a lot of running around to do to get ready."

Clare's eyes opened incrementally as she realized he was saying yes. Suddenly she was all business, sitting up straight, she pushed her shoulders back instead of moping against the door. "Oh, Dad. I can do anything you need help with."

"You promise?"

Clare nodded her head so quickly that her eyes blinked.

"Then yes, we can move to Dickens."

In a quick rush of squealing excitement, she unclipped her seat belt, launching herself into Julian's open arms. "Thank you, thank you, thank you, Daddy. Now we can get a dog and a pony like I ride at Creekside. And I can take the special classes that Avery is going to with that lady we met the other day. Miss Miller."

Julian's brain practically skidded to a halt thinking about the attractive teacher he had literally run into that morning. Or rather who ran into him. He still felt her soft skin in his hands, and his brain wouldn't let go of the light bouquet of what he assumed was her shampoo. He'd have to figure out a way to discourage Clare from the intramural program.

But that challenge was for another day. When he returned to BarrSoren after lunch, Julian would give the good news to Dane and immediately enlist his help in finding a place for them to live.

Half an hour later, despite a belly full of hot dogs and potato chips, Clare ran into the arms of Mari Rutger, nearly bowling the athletic equestrienne over. "My daddy says we can move to Dickens."

"Well, hi Clare. What's got you all wound up?"

"I'm excited 'cause Dad says we can move here. I can have a dog and a pony."

Mari looked over his daughter's head, winking at him before responding again. "Wow! That's great news."

Julian suppressed a laugh at Mari's enthusiasm as he

wondered whether Dane had told her about their business dealings and turned to his daughter.

"How about you give me a hug so I can get back to my meeting." Julian watched as Clare seemed reluctant to release her hold on Mari's waist before turning to him. "I love you, honey. Be good for Mari while I'm gone."

"Ooooo-kay, Dad." She rolled her eyes at him and then seconds later she dashed in through the open barn door.

"Hey," Mari stepped up to Julian, giving him a quick hug. "This is great news. Dane was so excited last night as he filled me in on all the ideas you two were floating about educational programming. It's a win–win for all of us."

"I'm thinking that Clare's getting the best deal. New friends, new house, a dog, and a pony." Julian shrugged, holding hands palm-side up. "And here I thought she would hate the idea of moving."

Mari gave him a hearty laugh that seemed to start at her toes and work its way up. "Hello, Earth to Julian. She's getting a dog and a pony. What eight-year-old girl wouldn't want that?"

"All right, I've got to go. Please send Dane a text to tell him I'm on the way for our two o'clock meeting."

Throughout the fifteen minutes it took for him to reach the office, Julian's head was spinning over the immediacy of how to handle the to-do list he had just agreed to. Phone calls needed to happen immediately, especially to Clare's school. And that's as far as he got. His brain refused to cooperate.

Parking his Jeep in the shade of a large maple tree, he took a deep breath. Followed by four more. In, out. Clearing his head and his lungs, forcing himself to relax. *You're a grown man. One with bucketloads of money. You don't have to do anything. You're going into that building to call your attorney. Not only is Reena a shark of a lawyer, but she has your best interests in mind.*

"Phew." Having settled the stress that had been squeezing the air from his body for the past few days, Julian felt much better. No one on this planet was more important to him than his daughter. If she had declined the move to Dickens, he would have respected her wishes and worked in a remote partnership with Dane. But since she had suggested the change, his body felt light and his heart was happy as he walked past Lena at the front desk, smiling broadly as he waved to her.

Julian wove through the physical labyrinth of the BarrSoren headquarters, arriving at the executive suite. No sooner had he pulled open the large glass door than his friend stepped from his personal office, a smile plastered across his face. Resisting the urge to answer any questions regarding his conversation with Clare, Julian lobbed out his own, loudly.

"For crying out loud, Rutger. Where can a guy get his own personal office in this joint?" Both men bellowed with laughter, sharing a congratulatory hug before Dane turned Julian around to find a piece of paper hanging from a door thirty feet across the large anteroom. In bold letters, traced with orange highlighter was his name on the hastily created sign: Julian B. Thomas.

Dane dropped a set of keys into his right hand and clapped him on the back. "Welcome, partner."

SITTING across the table from Roni and Mari, Anna couldn't believe how easily she had slipped into friendship with the younger women. Granted, the gap was less than ten years—the same as it had been for her and April. She smiled as thoughts of her other friendship filled her heart. April Stoneman was a very good woman and a loyal friend. Anna was excited for her to meet these women before she and her husband, Peter, returned to South Carolina for the winter. If only Jeanette was still in New York. It would be a great get-together.

"Hey," Mari waved her hand in front of Anna's face. "Are you still hanging with us or somewhere off in la la land?" Her warm laughter snapped Anna back to the present.

"Yes, sorry. I was just thinking about how much my old friend April will like you two." Her cheeks warmed with a blush. "They're supposed to visit before they head back to Charleston."

"They?" Roni cocked her head.

"Yes. Her husband Peter. They stay in her house in Albany during the summer months unless they're traveling elsewhere. But they don't head back down the coast until hurricane season is pretty much over."

"Well, it'll be great to meet them." As Roni stood from her chair, she placed her hand on the small of her back. "Ugh, aching back. I must need a new chair in the office."

"Are you sure it's your chair?"

For a second Anna thought she'd spoken her thoughts out loud, but then she saw Roni's eyes skewer Mari with a questioning look. "What choo' talking about Willis?" Her silly imitation of Gary Coleman fell out of her mouth like she used it every day, much like Anna's own brothers.

Anna chuckled inside as Mari did the friendship two-step. "Girl, I'm not talking about anything. I've got to get back to the farm. My newest student has a lesson at one fifteen."

"Newest student. Posh," Roni waved her hand at Mari. "Are you and your hubby tag-teaming that handsome guy?"

"I have no idea what you're talking about." Mari covered her face. "Now, really, I have to run. Glad you could join us today, An."

Before Anna could push her chair in, Mari was out the front door of Dorrit's with a box of freshly baked deliciousness tucked under her arm.

"I am so glad we didn't walk over from the office," Roni muttered as they stepped onto the sidewalk.

Anna looked up at the sky, thinking that Roni was referring to the weather. But the sky was a brilliant robin's egg blue without a single cloud. "It's a perfect day."

"Indeed. But I have a perfect backache and can't

imagine walking that far right now." Roni opened her driver's door of the Mini Cooper.

When they left the office earlier, Anna was shocked when Roni tapped her key fob, causing the horn of this car to chirp at them. She really expected someone as tall as Roni to drive an SUV, not a saucy little turbo charged station wagon.

"Do you and Mari always tease each other like that?"

"Like what?" Putting the car into gear, Roni checked the sideview mirror before pulling out. "Mari and I are just the sister that neither of us had growing up. You wanna become our triplet?"

If Anna hadn't already liked this woman, the quick and clean way she shifted gears of the Mini would have won her over. Growing up, all her older brothers had driven standard transmissions and insisted that she had to learn. So, she had—and Anna assumed that Roni's older brothers had been influential in developing her skill, also.

"Why, how sweet of you. You two ladies have been very generous to me already. So yeah, sis!"

Roni was still laughing as they pulled into the parking lot at BarrSoren. "To answer your question, I wasn't teasing Mari earlier. When she and Dane put their heads together, nobody is safe from their persuasion. But fingers crossed that it worked this time."

"What do you mean?" The women had stopped in the shade of an intricately colored, and huge, wind sail.

"Julian. He's not just an old friend of Dane's. He's a very talented programmer."

"Julian Thomas?" Anna must have telegraphed her

confusion judging by how quickly Roni jumped back into her explanation.

"That's the one. Remember, BarrSoren is a computer programming company. The Academy is brand new this year. Dane was tired of losing the best programmers because they didn't think the small school district here could give their kids the education that ones in Boston and New York City could."

"Yeah, I know. It was part of my interview. I'm pretty excited to work with these kids. But what does it have to do with Julian?"

"Oh, that's simple. Dane has asked him to join the company." Roni pulled out her phone. "Cripes, now I'm going to be late."

Anna had to trot to keep up with Roni's incredible walking stride. "Are you supposed to be telling me this personal stuff about this guy?"

"Sure, it's no secret. Dane told a mess of the department heads about it at a meeting. Believe me, Anna. The guys in this company can be total gossips. Watch what you say around them." Roni's laugh kept Anna company on the way back to her office.

Since Anna knew she was prone to talking to herself, she made sure to securely close the door before starting work. Dropping into the chair, she lifted the cover of her laptop, opening a world of research capabilities. "Who is this Julian guy anyway?"

CHAPTER EIGHT

November, Current Year...

A text from her brother Andrew had Anna looking for a chair to sit in. "The holidays already?" She slid back into the deep cushions of the overstuffed recliner her father preferred to use with every intention of sending back a lengthy declination. But after several minutes of never-ending single finger typing and multiple changes, she gave up and tapped the phone icon by his name at the top of the text. Of course he picked up on the first ring.

"Why?" It was all her tired brain could spit out.

"Hey. Nice to talk to you, too." Andrew's laughter filled her ear. "Why what?"

"Andrew don't play with me. Why do you want me to host Thanksgiving?"

"Let's see. You're an exceptional cook who is refusing to come back to Albany and Dad is now living with you.

Our families want to be with both of you. And you know what we promised Mom, so don't go all single woman cranky on me, now."

"Single woman cranky? You're a jerk. Do you talk to your wife this way? Or any of your sisters-in-law?" She took a deep breath before continuing. "And if you tell me not to get prick-aly, I will poke your eyes out the next time I get close to you."

"Oh Sis, I really miss seeing you. When are you moving back?"

"Sorry, Andrew. No time soon. I love this job. The kids are great, the town is sweet and safe, and I'm making friends."

"I'll tell you one thing, it sure is great to hear that smile in your voice. Not to mention that it's been a few years since I heard you say that you love your job."

"Thanks." Anna's eyes filled with emotion at his comment. "Listen, I'm not yet sure of my own plans for Thanksgiving. Give me a few days to mull it over and I'll give you a call back."

"Okay, kiddo. I will be nagging you in four days if I haven't heard back on this. Tell Pops I said hi. Where is he, anyway?"

Anna started laughing as she realized that her brothers knew nothing of the "new life" their father was living away from Albany. "Um, he's at the Dickens Community Center. Water Aerobics Class."

"Wait a minute. Is he wearing one of those skull caps and twirly dancing in circles in the shallow end of a pool?"

"I'm not answering anymore questions. You want to interrogate him, call back around six-thirty tonight. I love you, brother. Gotta go."

She disconnected the call before he could extract any more information from her. Besides, she needed to get to the academy long before her afternoon session started. One of the parents had suggested she teach the kids about being self-sustaining, starting with an indoor garden. And Anna being Anna took that idea and ran with it—even if she generally killed more plants than she managed to save.

As she slid into the seat of her car, Anna glanced at her phone. "Crap. Garrett is delivering that stuff in less than ten minutes, and he doesn't know where I want it." She threw the silent car into gear and peeled out of her driveway. Fingers crossed the boys in blue of Dickens finest were all inside the station and not running a radar detector. Once she made it through the main part of the village, she stomped on the accelerator, pulling into the BarrSoren parking lot at two-oh-two.

"Please tell me no!" She parked at her usual spot near the charging stations and dashed across to the mountain-sized delivery of supplies, where she found a hastily scribbled note jammed between a bag of potting soil and the thick plastic bands holding it all in place.

Hey—tried calling your phone but no answer. Jack Archer called for an emer-

gency delivery of shavings and antibiotics for a downed heifer. Sorry—Garrett

Staring at the thirty bags of soil, Anna wanted to cry. *How am I going to get all this inside?* She leaned against the stack, burying her face in her arms to help her think.

"Everything okay?"

Anna spun quickly, her arms outstretched for protection, slamming into the rock-hard side of Julian.

"Ow. Bloody hell. Why'd you hit me?" He jumped backward as if he thought she would take another shot at him. Then he started laughing while pointing at her. "Looks like you've got a leaky bag."

Anna looked down at her pink and black plaid, long-sleeve cotton blouse to find dark, wet dirt covering her belly and running down the front of her jeans. *Can this get worse?*

"Is this for the survivalist project you're starting today?" Julian waved toward the offending pallet of dirt and other supplies. "How did it get here?"

"I asked Garrett Brown at Dickens Seeds, Feeds, and Other Outdoor Needs to deliver it. But our schedules got out of whack because of a cow over at Pickwick Acres."

"That Jack Archer's a funny guy." Julian's chuckle surprised her. "Apparently he caught the same bug to be a farmer that Dane did."

"What do you mean? Dane has lived here for years."

"Oh, no. Dane spent summers here. But he grew up in Manhattan. When he and Mari reconnected, he decided that running a horse farm was much better than riding the subway."

"I can't say as I blame him." Anna shook her head slightly. "Listen, I'd love to stand here and talk but this dirt isn't going to move itself inside." She held her hand up as she started to walk toward the building. "See you later."

Anna made it about ten feet when Julian shouted, "Where are you going?"

"Where does it look like? Into the building to look for a cart or wagon." She couldn't prevent the "oh, duh" sarcastic tone in her voice.

"Or you could try this." He wiggled his phone in front of her, pressing the speaker button. "Hey, Dane? Have we got a maintenance crew on site with a pallet jack?"

"Yes, we do. The office is in C-11, but hold on a sec."

Anna moved closer to the phone, hiding her crossed fingers behind her. No way did the owner need to know that she'd messed up on this.

"Julian, I've got him on the line. Tim, can you help Julian move something?"

"Sure can, Mr. Rutger. Are we talking about that delivery that showed up out front?"

Anna groaned, causing Julian to stare at her. Then he started to smile. "That's the one. As I understand it, a sick cow pulled rank over Ms. Miller and Garrett dropped the load before she got here."

Various ninja moves flashed through her mind as she

pictured a round house kick to Julian's jaw, knocking the phone out of his hand at the same time.

"Yeah. Well, she's still adjusting to rural life. Tim, can you go out front to help? And Anna, next time give Garrett directions to the side door in your wing." She hung her head in exasperation as Dane's laughing continued until Julian ended the call.

THE MINUTE JULIAN returned to work he noticed Anna leaning on a stack of what appeared to be bags of potting soil, peat moss, mulch, and if he wasn't very mistaken, a pair of straw bales that had arrived while he was at the dentist. Clare had taken the bus home with Avery and Ryan, so she was at Victorian Hall. Fortunately for Julian, both of Syd Smith's kids were taking the same afterschool class as Clare, leaving him with extra quiet time in his office to work on some of the new programming. The very last thing he expected was to find the curvy form of Anna Miller semi-collapsed on the delivery.

Based upon her reaction to him checking on her, she did not appreciate his inquiry. I mean, how else is a guy supposed to perceive a woman practically cracking his ribs? She's a fiery one, that's for sure, but he hadn't planned on running into her, let alone tangling with her quick temper. Not for the life of him could he figure out why Clare liked the woman so much.

When Tim from maintenance showed up to move the pallet, Julian opted to leave him to handle the problem. And he'd stayed in his office for the next three hours. Peacefully listening to Pavarotti recordings while his fingers flew across the keyboard effortlessly, his mind traveled several lines of code faster than he could type. Until he looked over the top of his monitor, out the window, across the darkened grassy square, and into another part of the building.

There she was, talking to the kids. Her head thrown back in laughter, her ponytail bouncing happily as her neck arched from the collar of the adorable pink plaid shirt she had on. Unlike many circumstances where a group of students were together, Julian saw no horsing around. Each of the students stared up at her, seemingly transfixed by what she was doing and saying. At one point, she held up her arms, the sleeves of her shirt rolled above her elbows, her hands covered with dirt. Seconds later, the kids did the same thing.

When Anna bowed her head, everyone in the room raised their hands higher, swaying their arms, wiggling their fingers. Then they plunged their hands into the boxes of dirt in front of them. As Julian watched the interaction from afar, he realized why his daughter, and the other children, liked this teacher so much—she was one of them. Lowering herself in age, and raising them closer to adulthood, she taught as if she were their equal.

"Whoa. How did I not see that before now?" He

shook his head at his rhetorical question. For reasons he was unwilling to contemplate, Julian knew he'd avoided her since the first day. And some days his gut sensed she was doing the same thing.

But his body threw a traitorous monkey wrench into his plan to pretend Anna was inconsequential to him; just the sight of her triggered a lust he hadn't felt in years. A mind numbing, sleep losing, embarrassment inducing desire that he'd kept hidden away for a very long time.

Julian stared at the computer screen for a few minutes, trying to concentrate on the words in front of him. But even as Luciano's incredible tenor crested with emotion during *Nessun Dorma*, he couldn't find the energetic flow normally created within him at the bold ending of the song.

His wandering eyes returned to the window once more. This time he caught sight of Clare hugging Anna's waist. The teacher had one hand on his daughter's arm, the other rested on her head. But the act of affection was short lived as each of the children took turns embracing their teacher.

Moments later they were pulling on coats, some picking up backpacks, all of them leaving the room as Anna ran her hand over the light switch, effectively shutting down Julian's distraction. He took his cue, logged off his computer, and headed out front to where Clare and the Smith kids would meet him.

"HAVE you ever watched her interactions with them?"

"What are you talking about?" Dane cocked his head at Julian.

"Anna. Have you ever seen how well she gets along with the kids?"

"No, but she's a teacher. Has been for years. Isn't getting along with kids sort of a prerequisite?"

"Come on, Dane. Did you ever have a teacher you liked so much that you hugged her? In front of the other kids? The kids she had in the survival class last night stood in line to hug her on the way out of the door."

"First of all, yes. When I was in sixth grade, if Miss Wentworth had asked me to lick her shoes, I would have. But then she cheated on me and got married to some football player for the Jets."

"Ha, ha, ha. Good looking but she had bad taste?"

"Wait a minute, how do you know this about Anna and the kids?"

Julian swung his hand toward the window. "Her lab-slash-classroom is right over there. And it's November, so it's pretty much pitch black by the time they finish at six thirty. If I'm on driver duty but opt to be working here, I can't help but look over there because there's a bunch of activity catching my eye."

"Oh. Just so you know. There are two labs and four classrooms. I've sort of been planning for the Academy for a while now." Dane walked closer to the window and turned to Julian. "But I'm still a little confused about what you're saying. Are you inferring there's something bad going on?"

"No. I haven't been able to figure out why Clare is so taken with her, but now I know."

"Because of a hug? Buddy, I think you're the one who could use a hug. And let's face it, Anna is an attractive woman. You did notice that, right?"

"How did this turn around to be about me? I'm trying to tell you that the kids like her because she's just like them. You should have seen them all last night; dirt up to their elbows and smiles on their faces. And I mean hers, too. I think she comes down from the great teacher soap box and treats the students with respect." Julian stared past Dane, looking at the other wing of BarrSoren. "I'm saying that I think she's a good teacher."

"Glad to hear that, sir. I sure as hell don't want you moving back to the big city." Dane gave Julian's shoulder a squeeze. "Now, can we talk about the holidays?"

"Which one?"

"Did you get enough sleep last night? You're acting awfully loopy today. Thanksgiving. It's only a few weeks away. Will you and Clare be in town? We'd like you to join us on the farm."

"Oh, wow. Honestly, I hadn't given it any thought. If I ask Clare about your offer, there's no way she'll be willing to go elsewhere. So, the answer is yes—we'd like that."

Dane laughed loudly when Julian finished. "Man,

you are in rough shape today. Are you sure you weren't thinking about hugging Ms. Miller in your sleep?"

"Why would you think that? No, absolutely not. She's my kid's teacher. Besides, we're like oil and water. And it's not going to matter how much you shake that bottle—we are always going to be pulling apart." Julian scooped a pad of paper from his desk and started toward the door. "I'm pretty sure we have a meeting with the department heads in about five minutes."

But Dane wouldn't let up on the teasing and kept laughing at Julian's response—especially when he said nothing at all.

CHAPTER NINE

Mari: Meeting at 2-Sisters Kringle

Roni: Day?

Anna: Time?

Mari: Now, you pair of gomers. I need some breakfast.

Anna was still shaking her head at the interaction with her friends when she parked her car. *Is this what it's like to have sisters?* If so, she was happy that these two women had found her.

The bells hanging on the entrance gave off a surprisingly soft and melodic jingle as Anna stepped through the glass door. She stood for a moment to draw in the magical scent of freshly baked goods. *Ahhh, it's like a warm hug from your gramma.* She opened her eyes and looked to her left when she heard a couple of quick finger snaps. Roni was holding her hand aloft and winking, an unspoken threat to repeat the command for Anna to pay attention and join them at the table.

"We started without you." Mari stated the obvious while glancing down at the plate of kringle sitting on the table.

Fortunately for Anna, there was also a carafe of coffee and a clean cup waiting at the third seat.

"Here's the deal," Mari said. "I have a Thanksgiving emergency."

"I thought you said you were hungry." Roni folded her arms over her chest, emitting a loud harumph. "I was at work, you know." The blondish brunette leaned back in her chair, subconsciously rubbing her belly.

"What's the emergency? I'm pretty sure it falls on the last Thursday of the month every year." Anna winked at Mari, teasing her.

"Let's start with the fact that my husband seems to think that our house can hold over forty people. And that I can cook for that many of them."

"So, what's the problem?" Anna shook her head in confusion. She honestly didn't see the problem because her immediate family totaled close to that number. Every gathering they had required three days of cooking or job assignments.

"You could be me. Jon and I are expecting half of Long Island to come. To hear my mother describe it, all of North Massapequa is excited about touching this little nugget before he or she makes their debut." Roni's hand returned to rubbing in slow circles.

"And what about you? Is the entire city of Albany coming?" Mari's angst seemed to increase at Roni's quip.

"That's what my brothers want but I haven't made a commitment yet. I have no idea where I will put all of them to eat, let alone sleep."

"Hey, I have an idea." Roni's head snapped up from staring at her growing belly. "Let's have a big community meal. We can string tables down through your barn, end to end."

"Ewe, you want to eat cream sauces and mashed potatoes in my barn with all those flies? You do know they fly low and slow as the cold weather moves in, right? Suffering flies are so gross—I don't even eat PB and J out there. But you might be on to something."

"Aren't most restaurants closed or already fully booked? I mean, there's always Chinese." Anna stifled her laugh after seeing the stink eye Mari and Roni gave her.

"The Community Center. We can fit at least one hundred people in there. They use it for big gatherings all the time. I'll reach out to Gabriel Reyes to find out if it's available before we start planning." Mari stood from the table, excitement radiating from her. "By the way, Anna. some of your students will be there. I know that Dane invited Syd Smith's family, along with Julian and Clare. Sorry, no day off for you."

Thinking about their interaction from the night before, Anna hoped that neither of them could see her pulse speed up at the mention of the most handsome man in Dickens. She didn't mind spending the day with Clare, but she wasn't sure how she'd manage to avoid the girl's father while stuck inside with him for hours.

"No worries. My kids are all great." Anna dug in her purse for cash to pay her share of the bill, finally pulling a ten out for Mari.

"Nah. Next time you cover it. But will one of you do me a favor and puh-leeze drop this off in Dane's office? No way do I want the delicious baked goods of the Sorensen sisters calling to me from my kitchen counter."

Roni took the box and started for the door. "I've got to go. My chain-gang driver of a boss will meet me at the door with piles of work if I don't get back soon." She raised an eyebrow at Mari, but the other woman didn't fall for the intentionally exaggerated slight about her husband. "Anna, I'll meet you in the parking lot."

As each of them went about their business, Anna's mind traveled back to Julian. She hadn't realized he was hiding a solid body underneath the starched shirts he always had on. But when her arms accidentally connected with his ribs, there was no mistaking that he was a wall of man.

"Ya know, chick. It might be time for a quick overnight to Albany to check up on your house. Maybe you can connect with one of your 'ever on-call' single male friends." Even in her head that sounded lame. *What am I now? A sailor with a doxy in every port?* But she knew there had been a drought in her personal life and the father of one of her favorite students had become a mirage of a condensation-dripping pitcher of clear, cool water. She'd never had a relationship, single night or otherwise, with the parent of a child in her classroom. Surely this small town was not the place to change that personal rule.

Resolved to satiate her needs elsewhere, Anna knew she could stay away from Julian. After parking her car and walking to where Roni waited, both women started toward the front door of BarrSoren. With her concentration on the overwintering plant beds to either side of the opening, she didn't realize that Roni had been speaking to her.

"Thanks."

Anna felt the carboard box pressing into her stomach. "What?"

"I was just telling you that my bladder was not going to make it to the ladies' room near my office. Please take that to the executive suite."

Anna looked down at the box, wondering how she had missed the conversation with someone walking by her side. "Uh, yeah. Sure. It's on my way to my wing of the building." Roni gave her a quick hug and scooted into the facilities, leaving Anna standing there.

Minutes later she pulled open the heavy door on the anteroom of Dane's office, noting the brass plaque mounted on the wall across the room. *Julian B. Thomas.* Anna's heart skipped a beat. She did not want him to find her delivering the box full of treats. With no receptionist available, she placed the box on a dark wall-side credenza about halfway between the two offices.

A soft click behind her caused Anna to spin around in fright, with her arms up and ready to defend herself.

"Whoa, Put those things down." Julian chuckled as he pointed to her balled up fists.

"Where did you come from? And why are you always sneaking up on me? Are you following me?" She felt her temper spike when a smile spread across the contours of his face.

He placed his hands over hers, lowering them to her sides, further igniting her confused emotions toward this man. "The first answer should be obvious. My office." He pointed over his shoulder to the now open door behind him. "Secondly, your inference that I arrive in your perimeter unannounced with frequency is inaccurate. And rest assured, I am not following you, or anyone else for that matter."

As she stared into his sable orbs with the impossibly perfect sweeping eyelashes, her fingers mentally scraped the marble edges of a very deep pool. *Oh no. This is why you were going to stay clear of him.* "I'm sorry. I don't know why I act like this around you." *Liar, liar, pants on fire! You do, but no way will you ever be telling him that he is totally distracting and absolutely lick-a-licious.*

JULIAN WAS thankful for the late afternoon lesson that Clare had at Creekside Academy. There was no way he wanted to be anywhere near the business offices or school classrooms at BarrSoren. He needed fresh air and some hard work to banish his increasing thoughts about Anna. Somehow, he had managed to stumble upon her earlier in the day, and his mind wouldn't let go of her memory ever since.

"Hi, Clare. Hi, Julian," Mari shouted to them as she stepped out of the grain room about halfway down the seemingly never-ending row of stalls.

"May I ride Snowman today?"

Julian and Mari looked at each other in surprise at Clare's request.

"What about Ginger, or Cupid?"

"Nah. They're just ponies. And I'm in third grade now. I'm not a little girl anymore."

Julian averted his eyes from Mari's reaction to his daughter's pronouncement before he burst into laughter. Since the move to Dickens, Clare had matured a great deal, offering to help in the house and interacting with many new friends. And while he missed the huggable appendage she had left behind, Julian was happy to see her blossom.

Mari's phone pinged in a holster on her hip. "Clare, why don't you go sit in the lounge to put on your boots and helmet. I'll be right there after I take care of this." She held the phone up in explanation.

After a flurry of texts, Mari returned the candy apple red device to its home, snapping the heavy cloth covering of her jacket over it. "Sorry, Julian. Just working out some Thanksgiving details with the ladies."

"Speaking of which, let me know what I can bring. I don't want to step on anyone's toes regarding traditional recipes, but I can hoist a cooler full of pretty tasty beverages—both alcoholic and non."

There was something about Mari's presence that helped him relax. Or maybe it was the unmistakable barn bouquet of green hay, pine shavings, and liniment that he found soothing. Much the way the aromatics of wellness salons reached out to him, the warmth of vanilla, sandalwood, and cinnamon transported his mind back to his mother's kitchen during the winter holidays when he felt loved and safe. When he was around the horses, and Mari by extension, his shoulders would loosen, and laughter was more inclined to work its way up through his chest and out into the air. "Is there anything I can help with?"

"Here in the barn or on Thanksgiving?" Mari threw her head back in a gusto-fueled laugh. "There's nothing to do here except bring the horses in, and it's too early for that. As far as Turkey Day, I need to get the head count from Roni and Anna before I can make any decisions. But thanks for asking."

"Mari? Are you coming?" Clare's plaintive call floated up the aisle from the rider's lounge.

"Yep, on my way. Gotta go, my client is calling." Her frequent chuckle kept Julian company for a minute after she disappeared from view.

Anna. The minute Mari mentioned her name, heat flushed through Julian's nether regions. The peace and joy he'd found in the agricultural environs gave way to lust. *Seems like I can't get away from her.*

With no reason to stay at the farm, Julian decided to go home. Surely there was a mind-numbing household chore he could perform to fill the next few hours at the house he was currently renting. Slowly, he backed his car from the parking area outside the barn and started the ten-minute drive to Dickens. As he traveled the winding roads, his only company was the brown and gray stalks representing the once thriving greens of summer flora, and his thoughts. *How do I stop them from going back to her again and again?*

Just as he was about to switch on the radio to fill his ears, he caught sight of a small red car parked in the high weeds surrounding a run-down farmhouse. As the driver's side door opened, he slowed his car to a crawl, eager to learn who would step from the vehicle. When the deep green puffer jacket Anna had left her classroom in the night before appeared, Julian slammed on his brakes.

What is she doing? It couldn't possibly be safe near that house. Without thinking clearly, Julian pulled into the overgrown driveway and jumped from his Jeep as she dropped out of sight.

"Anna!" His voice flew through the air as he pushed his way against dead burdocks and nettles, their once vibrant flower heads attaching themselves to the sleeves and front panels of his flannel overshirt. "Anna?"

Just as Julian reached the front porch, she popped up

out of a tangle of prickers, her face and the back of her hands covered in bleeding scratches. "Are you okay?"

"Julian? Why are you following me again?" He saw her eyes squint in consternation as she perched her hands on her hips. "Can't I go anywhere without you finding me?"

"I wasn't following you. I was driving home and noticed the car parked by a collapsing house. And you got out of the car. Seconds later you disappeared. I was afraid you'd fallen in a well or old pit." Julian's voice got louder with each sentence; his indignation piqued by her misassumption of what he was about. "And now you're covered in blood. Look at yourself."

She rotated her hands in front of him. "Oh. So, I am. But they're nothing. Look at what I found." She pointed to the base of the stone foundation. "Old arrow heads, axe tips, and coins."

As she started to bend down, Julian wrapped his hand around her arm. "Stop it, Anna. We're trespassing."

"Pfft. *You* are trespassing, but I'm not. This is my house."

"What are you talking about? I thought you had a house in town with your dad."

Anna drew herself up, arching her back and tilting her head at him with a dose of sass that made him want to kiss her, right there, in the weeds. "Not that it's your business, Mr. Programmer Extraordinaire, but I bought this house from the county about a month after I moved here." With pursed lips and flashing eyes, she looked ready for battle.

Julian blinked at her a few times as his thoughts ricocheted between the uncontrollable urges his body was expressing regarding Anna, and what might have gone through her mind when she made the knuckleheaded decision to buy a structure that would be best suited for a giant bonfire.

"Good luck." He tipped his head in her direction and waded back through the dead plants to his car. Everything about Anna Miller had his internal fuses exploding, and he didn't know how to handle that situation, or her.

CHAPTER TEN

The next few weeks flew by for Anna. The weather in Dickens had been crisp and clean. The once brilliant-colored leaves fluttered to the ground, a crunchy blanket thrown over open space wherever possible, pushing most people into a raking frenzy before the first snow could fly. But not her. She spent as much time as she could with the contractor clearing her driveway and lawns. Then, they did a walk-through of the barns at the far end of the property, discovering a veritable farmer's museum of old dairy equipment, smaller items for tillage and planting, and even an old tractor that had the contractor salivating.

She found another reason to grin daily as she literally unearthed the hidden treasures of a long-ago lifestyle. But given her propensity for espresso and foamed milk, she wasn't interested in reenacting the life of the settlers, but she did respect the strength it had taken from them to survive.

"Whoa, heavy thinking there, woman." She laughed at herself as she opened the back door to the kitchen, the rusty hinges complaining loudly. Stepping into the large, square room, she surveyed the work the contractor had already completed, excited to see fresh sheet rock on the exterior walls and new wires poking out of the bank of outlets she'd requested.

Anna had to admit, when she first met with Henry Owens from Colonial Restoration, LLC, she was skeptical about his goal of having the ground floor ready by Christmas. But each time she arrived, there was surprising headway. And each day, she grew more excited about this very real step in her life.

Deep in thought, Anna squeaked in surprise when her phone pinged in her pocket. "Ut oh, I've been gone a long time. I hope Dad is okay." Retrieving the ever-attached device, an unladylike roar burst from her lips at the picture her brother Andrew had just sent to her. All four of the guys—Andrew, Austin, Adam, and Anderson —along with their wives and children, dressed in various pilgrim outfits, had cutouts of Anna and their dad taped on either side and a note in orange and brown letters. GOBBLE, GOBBLE, C U SOON!

Tears pricked the back of her eyes. No doubt she had the very best family. And there was also no doubt that she missed them all like crazy. Having her dad, George, with her in Dickens soothed the pain a little. But she ached for the combative love she shared with those four knuckle-heads. She responded to Andrew with a few hearts and blowing kisses emojis just before walking out to her car.

Stepping around the back corner, she looked up at the sound of a car driving by. *Julian.* A smaller arm waved happily from the back of the passenger side, putting a smile on Anna's face. Clare was quite chatty about her lessons and the schedule she kept at Creekside. Even if she hadn't been, Anna would have figured it out based upon the number of times she had seen Julian's Jeep go past. Whether it was live, or recorded on the security cameras she'd had installed, the man seemed to pop up in her life several times a week.

As she watched the vehicle disappear around a bend in the road, she found herself overwhelmed with thoughts about him. Ever since her first day on the payroll for BarrSoren, when she'd met him at Dane and Mari's house, this man and his daughter had been taking up more headspace than the average student–parent combo.

Clare was a generous, bright, and kind young lady, with a stunning knowledge base. But she wasn't pretentious. She was funny and seemingly unaffected by her father's professional success. And Julian? Where did she start with her thoughts about him? If she were talking to a therapist, she would describe him as quiet, clean, and well dressed—very unassuming, but not a pushover.

However, if she'd been hanging out with April or Jeanette, Anna would push the edges of polite with a few hubba, hubbas, followed by licking her lips and fanning herself. The man had an incredible body and was tall enough for her to wear any height heel she wanted to. He caused her pulse to race, and her lady parts to overheat.

Anna stood in the cool, late-autumn air allowing the breeze to chill her flushed cheeks, knowing that she was losing her own battle. Settling into her car, she made a decision.

> Anna: Are you busy?

> Mari: Nope, normal stuff. I'll be in the barn.

> Anna: Thanks. OMW

SHE HOOKED A LEFT out of her driveway before she could change her mind about confiding in Mari. She had met Julian nearly four months before, and she had questions. And needed advice. A few minutes later, her tires crunched over the gravel entrance to Creekside Riding Academy. As promised, Mari stood in the open doorway, wearing a warm greeting on her face.

"Hey."

The two women hugged.

"What's up? Are you okay?"

Anna stepped back from her warmth and nodded, words stuck in her throat. She wanted to scream, to laugh, to ask a thousand questions, but she could barely swallow.

"Nobody's around. Shall we have a cuppa in the lounge?"

Once they were both set up at the table with a steaming mug of dark, aromatic coffee, coats slung on the backs of chairs, Mari broke the silence.

"This is out of the norm for the you I have come to know. Out with it."

Anna stared at Mari's warm eyes a moment. "I'm not used to sharing my personal life with friends. I think it might have to do with growing up with all brothers—I had no one to confide in as a teenager. But," Anna looked at the coffee cup she held, "I just need to know about someone."

Mari canted her head but said nothing.

"Okay, Julian. It's Julian. I just need to know about Julian."

Her friend's response was instantaneous and explosive. "Bawahahaha! I can't believe it has taken you this long to open this conversation. What about him?"

"What should I know?"

"So, I'm not privy to his height, weight, IQ, or shoe size, if that's what you're looking for."

"Jeezus, you sound like Roni right now. Is he married?"

"Oh, so my girl's doing a little coy sniffing, eh?" Mari tipped her head. "I'll save you the painful part of asking me stuff and give you the condensed version. Julian and my husband have been friends for years—met professionally when they were both starting out in the tech world. He's from a small town in Connecticut, has a brother. His wife abandoned him shortly after Clare's third birthday and hasn't been seen or heard from since."

"What? How does a mother do that?" Anna's emotions surged for the hurt of a little girl growing up without her mom, threatening to surface as full-on tears. She'd lost her own mother in the last few years and missed her terribly.

"Let's face it, people have their -isms. As far as I can gather from conversations with Dane, Julian has been virtually celibate since then."

Anna drew up in surprise at what she said. "You want me to believe that a man that good looking hasn't had mad numbers of women trying to hook up with him?"

"I'm sure he has, but the problem for him is two-fold. First, he has an impressionable young daughter, and he feels his behavior should be circumspect. Secondly, it's difficult for him to know whether women are interested in him, or his money."

"What money? How much do programmers make?" In moments like this, Anna questioned her choice of occupations. *Does everybody make more money than me?* But in her heart, she knew that her choice to teach had come from her heart and had nothing to do with salary. At this moment, the confusing turn of the conversation had her shaking her head.

"An, are you serious right now?" Mari leaned forward, slack jawed. "You don't know who he is?"

"I know his name, that he's from Manhattan, and his daughter is sweet. As long as he's not a serial killer, what else matters?"

Mari put her hand on Anna's forearm. "Anna, Julian

is a very successful tech mogul, and a multi-millionaire. And with the programming he's working on with Dane now, they'll both be adding a few more zeros to their net worth. Did you not know that?"

"Why would I? Dane's just an ordinary guy. And lots of company owners are up to their eyes in hock. And besides, I don't need some man's money. I've done very well for myself without anybody helping me. Not even my family."

As her temper spiked, Anna vaulted from her chair, bumping the table and sloshing coffee on the laminate surface. *Does she think I'm after his money? Is that why he's so standoffish with me?*

"Calm down. And sit down."

"Well, I don't want you thinking I'm some old-fashioned gold digger."

"I don't. Look at who you're talking to. I wouldn't marry Dane until he agreed that this farm and the riding business remained in my name only, with no money from his company. I was very young when I married my first husband, and I never complained when he took control of my life in many ways. But I found out later that I had lost way more than just control of my finances. I gave up a good share of me, also." Mari glanced at the cup she cradled in her work-worn hands. "Believe me Anna, I understand how it feels to be a strong, independent woman. You and I wouldn't be such fast friends otherwise." Mari grew silent as she took their cups back to the K-cup machine for a refill.

"Do you think Julian has been acting so weird toward

me because of the money thing? I mean, in his eyes, I'm just a schoolteacher."

"Nope. I think he's drooling over you but doesn't know if he should ask his daughter's favorite teacher out on a date." Mari winked at her. "And it might be that you scare him...just a little."

"Oh, stop it!" Anna heard herself squeal like a teenager. "That big lug isn't afraid of me."

Both women finished their coffee, moving to the sink to tidy up as a team. When they turned to leave, Anna nearly fainted when she found Julian standing in the doorway, grinning.

AS EARLY DAWN light colored the sky with a soft pink on Thanksgiving morning, Julian knew his thoughts would keep him from sleeping any longer. In the brief four days since he overheard Anna's confession, his mood swung between happy and walking on air. An incredible high he'd denied himself for years.

Contemplating how to approach her for a date, he watched the sunrise, drinking coffee in the small kitchen of the white home he had been renting since August. From the moment they pulled in the driveway, Clare had been in love with the little cottage, insisting it looked like a gingerbread house.

The first time he entered the kitchen, Julian blinked his eyes at the time warp sensation. The lower seagrass cabinets, topped with a hunter green counter, complimented the white upper cabinets with a floral pattern running across the bottom of each of the doors. The island that dominated the room was white marble speckled with flecks of green. Even the curtains in the crowded space were seagrass. *Am I in the Brady Bunch house?* The old kid friendly television show was something he and Clare frequently watched together.

Before they had even unpacked their belongings, some sort of welcome wagon had arrived with hot food, something he really appreciated later when his daughter happily wolfed down the mac 'n cheese and a side of green beans. He secretly wondered if the women who handed them to him were parents of hard to please children.

As he looked around the cozy room, he realized that he'd struck gold when his friend talked him into visiting Dickens to consider working there. It was a welcoming town of warm people who took everyone at face value. They took care of each other, with children at the top of their list. Something Julian admired. And no one mentioned his wealth or his company. In Dickens, he could be a regular ol' single dad.

He took his second cup of coffee and sat in the living room, the only portion of the house with windows large enough to see the sun come up. With his feet propped up and a cheery crocheted afghan across his lap, he listened to the sounds of the house. The bones settled a little, the furnace whirred on, the metal along the baseboard made soft clinking notes as the warm water traveled through the cool pipes. As he drained the last of his coffee, brilliant, yellow sunshine crested the house across the street from him.

EVERYWHERE HE LOOKED in the bustling community center, mayhem ensued. To others it might just seem like a big family. To Julian, it was a madhouse. He chuckled to himself when he thought about the text he had received from Mari shortly after sunrise.

> 4 big birds going in. Snacks at noon, dinner at one. Don't be late. And don't respond. I won't answer.

Leave it to the woman who seemed to prefer her barn to her house to refer to hors d'oeuvres as snacks. Then again, this was Dickens, a wonky and whimsical place.

When a line of well-built men came through the door, spending an in ordinate amount of time hugging Anna, Julian felt the green-eyed monster stir in his body. She had yet to say anything to him since his arrival, opting instead to hug Clare and coo over the decorations pinned in her hair. With the crowd of people surrounding her, it seemed he would have to be happy with hearing her laughter from across the enormous room.

"What's got you scowling? You want some alcohol in that tankard of cider you're palming there?"

Julian considered denying his foul mood when he turned to Dane, but decided it was a perfect time to ask questions. "How many families did you invite? Half the town?"

"No, actually, I didn't. Just you, Clare, and Jessica."

"My landlady?" Julian thought about the petite woman with the rosy cheeks who made the greatest baked goods and seemed to move about the village magically.

"That's the one." Dane looked around the crowd. "All these people are mostly family of the ladies." Julian was already aware of his friend's way of referring to Mari, Roni, and Anna. "Apparently every sibling, aunt, uncle, and cousin of Anna and Roni have always been at the family table. This whole town loves Thanksgiving because it is the official start of our biggest season— Christmas and Hannukah."

"My daughter has been wiggling with excitement for weeks over all of it." Julian laughed as he raised his cider to his lips.

"She is going to love Racing Through the Snow."

"You mean like making snow angels? She's mentioned it."

"Oh no, my friend. Racing Through the Snow is our family's contribution to celebrating the holiday season. Out at the farm we have tons of people, horses and dogs come for the day, competing in gymkhana-style games, gallons of hot chocolate, hundreds of Ruth's butter cookies, a staggering number of Santa costumes, and we wrap it up with the Christmas Derby."

Julian stared at Dane, finally understanding why the man had left Manhattan.

"Racing Through the Snow is held on December twenty-third. Save space on your calendar."

Dane clapped him on the shoulder before gravitating toward the raucous group surrounding Roni and her husband, Jonathan Hawthorne. Instead of filling his head with names of people he wouldn't see after today, Julian opted to find a task in the kitchen with—among others—Mari, her mother, and Jessica.

Stepping through the spring-loaded double doors, enticing scents, and laughing ladies surrounded him, a true balm to his grumpy soul.

"Hey, you're looking a lot like Scrooge there, Thomas." Mari's familiar laughter wrapped her statement. "Do you want a cookie?" She grabbed a Christmas tree cut-out with green frosting and silver balls as her mother walked by with the tray of desserts.

"Thanks, but I'm saving my appetite for that magic." He pointed to serving bowls teeming with stuffing, orange-cranberry relish, and mashed potatoes.

"Good timing. We're almost ready to serve. You can help us carry out the rest." Mari bit off the top half of the tree cookie. "Have you seen Anna today? Talked to her or anything?"

"Nope. Far as I can tell she's avoiding me. And now she's got a reverse harem surrounding her." With the flush of embarrassment warming his cheeks, Julian looked away from Mari. *Cripe, I'm such a loser in the dating category.* "Who's the cougar with the younger adonis?"

"Do you hear what you're saying? Why are you using some worn out phrase for a woman? You sound like a jealous fool."

Julian stepped back in surprise.

"That's Anna's friend April and her husband, Peter."

"Tell me something, Mari. Does Anna know any ugly guys?"

"Seriously? You big goof. Are you jealous?" She made a face at him, lifting one eyebrow much like she often perched a hand on just one hip. "First of all, those are her brothers. And second of all, you heard directly from the horse's mouth that she's attracted to you. Now pick up that tureen of cream sauce and carry it out to the sideboard. Then go say hello." Mari shoved a steaming china dish into his hands and returned to stirring the gravy on the stove top.

"Yoo hoo. Julian." Just before he left the warm kitchen, Jessica sought him out. "Dear, you need to listen to Mari. You and Anna have a special connection and there's no time to waste. You don't want to miss the magic of Christmas in Dickens."

More confused than ever, Julian retreated quickly. He placed the tureen on a trivet, thankful he hadn't dropped the scalding dish. When he heard Anna's voice, he turned to find her walking toward him. Suddenly, his lips were dry, and his heart started pounding out a staccato in his chest. When she was less than a foot away,

Julian opened his mouth to speak, but she held her hand up in his face.

"Don't. You were eavesdropping on a private conversation." He reached for her hand but reeled in surprise as she tapped his nose with her index finger. "I think you suck!"

CHAPTER ELEVEN

———————

Thanksgiving turned into a miserable blur in Anna's mind. After nearly a week of deciding how to approach Julian, he showed up for the massive dinner she, Roni, and Mari had planned looking like he'd just stepped from the pages of Cosmo or GQ. No man had the right to be so devilishly handsome and so exquisitely tailored. Even his recently trimmed dark curls accentuated his dark eyebrows. And every time he laughed at what someone said, she could practically see the sparkles in his eyes float around the room.

After sharing greetings, hugs, happy tears, and love with her brothers and their families, along with April and Peter Stoneman, Anna found herself dragged into an equally vociferous group—Roni's relatives from Long Island. The two women bumped shoulders and meaningful glances each time one of the brothers became overly protective, knowing they could never outgrow being the cherished little sister.

Even though Clare had come racing over to Anna nearly an hour before, her enticing father hadn't even waved. Ever the multitasker, she kept a surreptitious eye on his every move, noting each person he spoke to—especially the women—until he disappeared into the kitchen.

When Julian reappeared carrying a serving dish, Anna decided it was time to ask him to sit by her, amid her family. Moments later she was about to issue her invitation when the man turned to face her. His look of surprise quickly morphed into one of smug arrogance, a glint of "she wants me" in his eyes. And that was the moment Anna's temper flipped.

After nearly an hour of having the pompous man ignore her, she'd maxxed out on his cocky personality. She gave the tip of his nose a rude tap and told him he sucked. Shocked by her own reaction, Anna stomped her way out the front door, with gasps and whispers her only accompaniment.

Over fourteen days later, Anna hid in the safety of her classroom working on semester-end projects with the children. Despite the negative interaction with Julian, she and Clare had remained a happy pair, including the day she divulged her big news.

A week after Thanksgiving, Clare arrived for the after-school program wiggling with excitement. Once the older students settled into a new project, Anna sat at the desk next to Clare.

"What's got you so excited?"

"I thought you'd never ask. And Daddy said I couldn't

barge into class and tell you." The young girl's breath came out as a shoosh of punctuation after the admission.

"Tell me what?"

"About Barrel." Clare stood from her desk, her expressive eyes wide.

"What's barrel?"

"My dog. Daddy got me a dog!" She jumped up and down, clapping her hands and giggling. "He's big and soft and fluffy, just like Avery and Ryan's dog. He's even the same color."

Anna rose to hug Clare. "This is so exciting for you."

"He's black, brown and red. He's called a mountain dog."

"A Bernese Mountain dog?"

Clare's head bobbed rapidly. "Yeah, that. His name is Barrel."

With the excitement of her news released, Clare looked at Anna. "Can I start my project now?"

"Sure. Come on."

Every day Christmas drew nearer, and the third grader regaled her with another Christmas story about Julian. At that point, Anna couldn't decide whether Clare was totally immune to what had happened on Thanksgiving Day, or if she was trying to patch things up between the two adults. The need to mend wary adults isn't something most eight-year-olds would recognize, but Clare was a very special child.

Anna moved about holiday preparations with her father, albeit woodenly. At least he wasn't peppering her with questions the same way Mari and Roni had. After dinner one night, George encouraged Anna to join him at the kitchen table to share a cup of tea.

"I saw what happened between you and Julian on Thanksgiving. I don't know why, but I'm not asking. All I am saying, my beautiful baby girl, is that you can't let one person steal your happiness. The most precious of holidays is almost here. We live in a town that is the essence of Christmas, surrounded by magical elves."

Anna took a long swallow of the cooling chamomile before answering. "I know, Dad. I'm trying."

"I want you to know that Jessica has mentioned your glum attitude to me a few times."

"Jessica? Why? What did she say?" Anna hadn't spoken to the famous baker since first arriving at the community center early Thanksgiving morning. But she knew that many people in town revered the joyful woman, suggesting she was related to Santa Claus and had magical powers. *What could she possibly know?*

"Interestingly, she reminded me of how blessed your mother and I had been in our lifetime together. But the funny thing is, I've never talked to Jessica about anything personal." Her father's lined face turned into a lopsided grin as he shrugged his rounded shoulders. "I don't know what to tell you, kiddo. But she was adamant that you and Julian had a deep love for each other. However, she said there was a fast-approaching deadline before that spark would fade. She was concerned about your stubborn personalities getting in the way of eternal happiness."

"Dad, are you hearing yourself? She barely knows me. I'm not stubborn."

George roared with uncontrollable laughter, cupping his daughter's arm to steady himself. "Oh, my girl, your Scottish roots run deep. Next thing I know, you'll be pulling a Braveheart move and racing into battle against all of us."

Anna waited for him to drink his tea before saying anything. "Since you brought up our heritage, I got great news from Henry Owens. He said the house will be ready for the first of January." She giggled when she saw diamonds dancing in her father's eyes.

"Hogmanay! Oh, child. There is no better way for you to start the new year. You can be your own 'firstfooter.'"

Anna thought about the ancient Scottish tradition about the first person crossing your threshold on New Year's Day being a sign of good luck. Smiling at her dad, she knew how much these traditions meant to him.

All her life, her father had reminded her of the late actor, Brian Denehy. With his football player persona of being big and simple, sporting a thick mustache, his physique was in sharp contrast to the soft voice he used with his family. And now, his handsome, ruddy face curved with joy for her.

"That's right, Dad. And I want you and the boys to be there with me."

George Miller stood from the table before bending down to hug his only daughter. "Child, it's time for this old Highlander to find his bed. We'll talk about the house tomorrow after we've helped with the preliminary preparations for the big rodeo they're doing at Creekside."

Over the next several days, and with newfound excitement in her heart, Anna found many reasons to embrace the growing fervor of her first Christmas in Dickens. Her father spent many of his days in classes at the community center—from his water aerobics to baking lessons with Jessica. Every day he had something on his calendar. Thinking back, Anna couldn't remember him being this busy without his family in tow.

Each day the countdown progressed closer to December twenty-fifth, they attended another event in town. From church concerts to school plays, along with honoring the miracle of the eight nights of Hanukkah at Congregation Etz Chaim—everywhere you turned, Dickens was alight with love.

On the twentieth day of December, BarrSoren Academy was officially on vacation until January seventh. This extended period of vacation allowed families undisturbed time with each other. But it also gave her students a block of time free from the stress of studying.

On the twenty-first of December, Anna and George did one last shopping trip to prepare for the entire family's arrival.

The twenty-second was Anna's day to race in crazy circles—finishing the decorations, wrapping baskets of cookies, squeezing in phone calls from April and Jeanette, and flopping into bed at ten at night, exhausted.

With a red sunrise on the twenty-third of December, Anna watched lazy snowflakes float to the ground. With her fingers crossed for Mari and Dane, she hoped the predicted storm would go elsewhere. Much to the delight of every kid in a fifty-mile radius, nearly two feet of the fluffy white happiness had already blanketed the area; they could wait until after Racing Through the Snow ended for more.

As the day grew brighter despite the overcast skies, the only thing Anna wasn't looking forward to was running into Julian. She knew Clare was participating in some of the contests being held both on and off horseback and she assumed he would be there also. Other than a few side glances in the village, no one had mentioned their Thanksgiving blow up, or the frightfully cold air that now acted as a buffer between them.

Maybe Jessica had been correct. Maybe the opportunity to become a couple had expired over the last few weeks. Maybe Anna would never know whether she and Julian had a true spark. A need beyond the physical.

"You're bloody morose about this. There are many other fish in the proverbial sea. And if you meet another one you find sexy, *you* will set the rules because you'll be living happily in your new home with no need to surround yourself with someone else's company."

Anna rolled her eyes at her own statement. "Idiot. You really miss how Mr. Computer Genius made you feel. And that's gone forever."

"YES, you can go to the Smith's today." Julian had planned on working from home while Clare and Barrel got to know each other. Since she would be with Sydney and her children, he saw no reason not to work in the offices of BarrSoren where he had a much bigger monitor. Eye strain was a serious downside to the amount of time he spent staring at a computer screen.

"What about Barrel?"

"What about him?"

"Mrs. Smith said I could bring him any time I wanted to."

Julian stretched his back and rolled his neck to release the stress building there. "Hang on." He pulled out his phone, texting Syd.

> Julian: Did you really say this monstrosity of a dog was welcome at your house?

> Sydney: LOL. It's like having bookends. Bring him along.

> Julian: Thanks, I owe you.

> Sydney: Don't say that. We've got a long vacation ahead of us and I have a ton of work piled up on my desk too.

Fingers crossed that the wizard of the company HR department didn't ask him to take care of all three kids and both dogs on the same day. How so many parents managed to juggle multiples was beyond him.

"Clare, time to load up. Mrs. Smith confirmed Barrel's invitation."

Two hours after leaving his daughter and her elephant-sized friend at Pickwick Acres, Julian's phone buzzed across the glass top of his desk, snapping him out of deep concentration. The small hairs on the back of his neck popped up when SYDNEY SMITH-ARCHER filled the screen.

"Julian. Come qui—" her voice became jumbled with static and background noise.

"Syd, what's wrong? Syd? Answer me." Her name disappeared from the screen, replaced by two words: Call dropped. Frantically Julian tapped the dark screen trying to get connected to her as his deepest fears burned a hole in his stomach.

After three tries, he gave up. Jamming his phone into his back pocket while he rammed his arm inside his jacket and pulling it on as he sprinted to his Jeep, various scenarios of Clare being kidnapped, trapped in a well, or falling to her death spun in his mind as he navigated the slippery roads to Pickwick, fifteen minutes from BarrSoren.

Swearing at the fresh snow which had fallen while he hunkered down in his office, oblivious to anything that wasn't code, he spun out of the parking lot. A mile later, his phone flashed with Syd's name but cut off after a single ring.

Stomping on the gas pedal, the backend of the sturdy vehicle slid to the right. Instinctively he knew he needed

to calm himself and slow down. But with two more interrupted calls from Pickwick, that was out of the question.

With his hands wrapped around the steering wheel,
Julian crouched closer to the windshield, peering through
the flying flakes, the rapid *clunk-thunk* of the wipers
across the surface the only sound in the car.

Rounding a sharp corner, the Jeep's tires lost contact
with the road, sending the SUV into a spin. After two full
careening revolutions, the car came to a stop just inches
from a massive oak tree.

Unnerved by how close he had just come to
orphaning his daughter, Julian slipped the Jeep into Park,
dropped his head to his chest, and released a long, deep
breath. *You idiot.* After a few moments, he engaged the
transmission and four-wheel-drive, slowly returning to
the snow-covered asphalt.

After what seemed like two hours, Julian pulled into
the long driveway of Victorian Hall at Pickwick Acres.
Parking his car, he squinted across the far side of the field
beside the barn at what he thought was people walking
toward him. He set out across the open property, his coat
flapping while his feet plunged into the snow, thankful
that he'd worn heavy boots that morning.

"Clare!" Julian bellowed at the group, causing several
heads to snap up and arms to wave in his direction.

"Daddy. Daddy."

After racing across the football field-sized pasture to
reach his daughter, Julian dropped to his knees as he
dragged her into his arms, burying his face in the faux fur
lining in the hood of her snow suit. Battling to control his

emotions, Julian ignored his daughter's wriggling protestations that he was squeezing her.

Satisfied that she was okay, he released Clare and rose from the ground, only just noticing that his coat was open, and he was cold. Zipping his jacket with numb fingers, Julian addressed Sydney. "What happened?"

"We were all collecting pine boughs because the kids wanted to make wreaths, when Barrel charged into the woods." Sydney motioned to the edge of the trees, behind which stood a steep incline. "Before I could grab her, Clare chased after him. Within seconds they had disappeared."

"I wasn't lost Daddy. Barrel needed my help catching a chipmunk."

"I've never seen a kid move so fast. And she didn't respond to us. I was a wreck, that's why I called you."

Julian stared at his friend's ashen face. "You need a new cell phone." His simple statement leaving her with wide eyes.

"I'm really sorry, Julian. I was so afraid she'd get hurt. Or worse. There are a few caves and cliffs up there." Sydney took a deep breath. "And I know you were so worried something like this would happen when she was with someone else."

Observing the moisture filling Sydney's eyes, Julian held no animosity over the unfortunate incident and couldn't allow her to bear all the responsibility. "That's okay, Syd. It's not your fault that Barrel decided to go all Scooby-Doo on you."

"Clare, don't ever do that again or your buddy will

stay home." He looked down at his daughter. "Do you understand?"

"Yes, Daddy." She wrapped her arm around the aloof dog.

"Now, I don't know about the rest of you, but I'm freezing." He blew on his cupped fingers for effect, engulfing his hands and face in a pocket of steam. "Wreath making will have to resume after lunch."

Dogs and kids charged through the snow, laughing as if the adults hadn't experienced a minor melt down. Once they were out of range, Julian spoke up. "Don't worry, I'll be taking the goofy one home after lunch."

"But she wants to make a wreath for the house."

Julian roared at her misunderstanding, his words finally coming out with a chuckle. "Not Clare. I mean that eighty-pound goof ball by her side."

"Great. Thanks."

Julian resisted the urge to hug the company's HR director, even though she'd become his friend.

A few days later, the remainder of Julian's worry about Clare washed away when he pulled up to the barn. Looking around, he couldn't believe the number of people already at Creekside Academy at such an early hour. Everywhere he turned, he saw trucks and trailers of all sizes and colors. Horses whinnied, with giant clouds of steam pouring from their nostrils as their shod feet clomped down ramps, and handlers patted their necks to calm them.

For all the times Julian had socialized in the private boxes at Belmont and Aqueduct Raceways, or any of the five polo clubs on Long Island, he'd never seen the actual handling of the horses. As Clare dashed into the barn to find Mari, Julian took a stroll through the rows of rigs. From one to the next, his mind silently analyzed how much money went into each one, even at an event as casual as this one, these were investments that cost tens of thousands of dollars.

"Lilleth, stand still, please."

Julian turned to find a mother braiding her daughter's hair by an open door on the front of a horse trailer, the young girl squinting at herself in the full-length mirror. He chuckled quietly witnessing the same thing he'd been through multiple times when Clare was younger.

Next to another trailer, he witnessed a kid in an over-sized Santa suit fall face first into soft snow while leading a golden yellow pony. Julian listened for a moment to see if the child was laughing or crying. Until the rascal gave the inert form a head butt, causing waves of giggles to float across the crisp air, punching up the excitement for the start of Racing Through the Snow.

Returning to the barn, Julian found Clare wrapped in a relatively form-fitting red and white suit. At least if she fell in the snow, Julian wouldn't have to worry about her being able to stand up on her own. As his daughter turned to collect her mount, Julian heard the voice of Mari's dad welcoming everyone to the fourth annual event, culminating with the last contest, the Christmas Derby.

The roar of voices from the crowd, their clapping muffled by countless pairs of oversized gloves and mittens, hovered over the valley as people made their way ringside. Whether they sat in the bleachers or personal camp chairs, most of the women wrapped themselves in fleece blankets, holding cups of steaming beverages. Everywhere he looked, he saw young and old alike noshing on fistfuls of Ruth Jessup's beautifully decorated butter cookies or enjoying breakfast kringles from the 2-Sisters Kringle and Fudge Shop food truck. And every person wore a smile.

At the sound of a familiar voice, he located Anna in the announcer's booth with Mari and her dad, Don Jessup. Julian grabbed the nearby fence rail as an over-whelming rush of desire at the sight of her laughing and gesticulating with the two, completely unaware he was watching. A thick braid slid across her ski jacket and her rounded cheeks glowed with the pink of chill. She was stunning.

"Dad. Dad!" Clare's shouting interrupted his stolen moment when Anna turned toward the sound of her voice, then quickly scanned the nearby crowd. Her ebul-lience instantly extinguished when her eyes fell on his. Whispering something to Mari, Anna moved to the far side of where Don was sitting, effectively blocking Julian's line of sight.

The joy in his day crashed and burned into the ground like a spiraling airplane, fully engulfed in flames and then snuffed out on the cold, snowy ground. The day he had listened to her private words with Mari, his heart had jacked so high with happiness that he'd had to cover his mouth. When she did discover him standing there, an unnerving dark shroud covered her eyes, making him wish he were anywhere but smiling at her.

Just now, that same darkness had come across her beautiful face once again, muting her exquisite cheekbones and fading spray of freckles.

"What do you need?" Julian tried to keep his tone gentle with his daughter. It wasn't her fault he'd been foolish and was now paying the price.

"Daddy, I need a partner for the three-legged race. Can you do it with me?" Her long lashes fluttered against her alabaster skin, tugging at his heartstrings.

"I think I'm too tall. My legs are so much longer than yours that I'll be lifting you off the ground." Julian noticed movement in the announcer's stand as the words came out of his mouth.

"Anna! Will you do it with me?"

Her eyes darted between father and daughter while Julian kept his fingers crossed behind his back. If she said no, the letdown would set his daughter's mood for the entire vacation.

"Sure. I can help you out."

Julian let out a long breath, the crisp air wrapping him in a brief fog. When it cleared, he smiled at his savior, mouthing a silent thank you. But instead of snubbing him, she nodded in response. Julian took it as a win and went about the day in a better mood.

After the enchanted main event, the Christmas Derby, spectators were singing a variety of carols as they hugged their neighbors and friends. As if on cue, the lazy flurries that had been dallying about all day called in reinforcements, laying a thick white covering on everything it could. Young children climbed into car seats, while adults quickly loaded horses and ponies onto trucks and trailers. The enormous holiday crowd dispersed in less than fifteen minutes, likely leaving the hosts secretly thanking the weather gods for holding off until the end.

Julian had just finished helping Dane, Mari, and her parents break down the announcer's stand and said his goodbyes. He gave his aged Jeep a chance to warm up a few minutes before putting the 4x4 into gear. The tires spun for a second until the differential slid into four-wheel drive and then he slowly made his way toward the road.

At the far end of where countless cars had left tracks in the snow, Julian discovered a small car barely noticeable in the dark of the storm. Pulling over, he went to check it out. Just as he was about to wipe the layer of snow covering the driver's side, the door opened, and Anna stepped out.

"About an hour ago your dad told me he was leaving. What are you still doing here?"

"We took separate cars in case he got too cold." Anna pulled her knit cap a little lower on her head as a strong wind came rolling through the valley. "I can't get mine to start."

"Okay, I can help. I've got jumper cables."

"No, you don't understand, it's an EV."

"Clare told me you drove a hybrid." He saw her head shake as she tugged the hat down again. "Okay, let me take you home."

"No!" Anna blinked frantically at him. "I couldn't put you out like that. Clare must be dying for dinner after being out in the cold all day."

"She went home with the Smith-Archer family. As I understand it, Jack's version of Green Acres is more fun than our house, especially since they encourage her to bring her dog."

"What good sports they are. Sydney must vacuum everyday anyway. By the way, Clare was very excited about Barrel even though you didn't take her back to Furry Bottoms to find a puppy."

"Well, since I'm cleaning the floor daily, I'll agree with your assessment. And the arrival of Barrel is a little more complicated than that. Sydney is friends with Linda Abernathy, and they were aware of our new guy needing a home. But he's not a puppy. He's more like an eighteen-month pony-sized wrecking machine." Julian stepped back a few steps, pointing to the sturdy SUV. "Come on, you're freezing. You can text Mari after your hands warm up."

Silently Anna returned to her car, grabbing her purse and a Ziploc bag of Ruth's cookies, returning to climb into the well-warmed vehicle.

Julian slipped it into gear but kept his foot firmly on the brake.

"I just have one thing to say." He looked at her, waiting for a signal for silence but none came. "I am sorry about what happened in the barn a few weeks ago." Not expecting acceptance, he let the car roll to the end of the driveway, turning left into the drifting snow-covered road.

Julian's heart jackhammered in his chest as he began the slow ride toward town. His left hand had a firm grip on the top of the steering wheel while his right one rested on the ball of the gear shift. Keeping his focus on the driving instead of the awkward silence that filled the car, he wished he'd driven her up to the farmhouse instead of rescuing the grouchy damsel.

When they were halfway to Dickens, Julian started his favorite pastime to cure boredom: designing complicated algorithms in his head. The challenge was to see if he remembered all the steps he'd created so he could write them down.

With his mind deep in his favorite playground, he nearly shouted in surprise when Anna's warm hand rested on the back of his. "Take this right. Third house on the left."

He pulled into the drive, trying to get her as close to the porch as possible in case the walkway was slippery. When he put the Jeep into park, she lifted his hand from the gear shift, wrapping it with her own, setting off fireworks in every part of his body. Not until he looked at her directly did she utter a sound.

"Apology accepted."

She slid out of the passenger-side door before Julian could unbuckle his seat belt. Seconds later, as a solid door kept her well secured, the porch light went out.

Julian squinted through the windshield, trying to

absorb what just happened. *Did she just say what I think she did?*

CHAPTER TWELVE

For the next thirty-six hours, Anna tried to absorb every sliver of joy that she could from her first Christmas in Dickens. She spent a joyful day filled with lots of laughter at Racing Through the Snow, ending it with a warm and peaceful moment with Julian. Anytime she was apt to start second guessing her statement to him, she stopped in her tracks and looked at her family. Big brother Andrew and his family had surprised both her and George by showing up there just before bedtime. Cursing the storm for delaying them, her brother squeezed them into the spare room of the saltbox, with plans to stay until the twenty-sixth.

Every time Andrew made the effort to be with them in Dickens, it only made her love for him grow. He knew this job was important to her, and at Thanksgiving he'd commented that their dad looked healthier since the move. She giggled wondering how often he would drop in once the farmhouse was ready. Afterall, he was months away from retirement and the house had five bedrooms and three bathrooms. Anna had to surmise that the original owners were either wealthy or had many children.

"Hey, An. Wanna go sledding?"

When she heard Andrew bellowing, Anna trotted down to the kitchen. "Where?"

"Pickwick Acres. Jack and I were talking about it over Thanksgiving. He says they've got a great hill on the other side of their woods." Andrew gave his head a weird shake as he lifted one cheek up to his eye in a bizarre wink. "And don't worry about sleds, we brought some."

"What about breakfast? Nobody's eaten a thing."

"No worries, we'll stop in town." He lifted his arms in front of his torso, snapping his fingers. "Come on, you guys. Let's get moving. It's Christmas time and we've got snow to play in."

Anna found herself caught up in the excitement produced by the biggest kid in the room. Looking across to the couch, she caught her father's smile at his oldest child's antics. "Dad, are you coming with?"

"Oh, no. Yesterday was enough outdoor time for this old rack of bones. You guys go while I do some prep work for tonight's dinner. Besides, maybe I'll be able to find a football game to watch."

Throughout the remainder of Christmas Eve and into Christmas morning, the unexpected visitors brought endless hours of laughter, soft conversation, and love to Anna's new hometown. Even though she'd been around Andrew's family for years, this was the first time she recalled such in-depth conversations with his children. Just because she was a teacher didn't mean she always listened to kids. And somewhere along the line, these two had grown from combative siblings to close friends thinking about colleges.

Shortly after they had wrapped up another meal of ham from the twenty-five-pounder Andrew had carved the night before, they all curled up in various spots throughout the living room. Some watched the annual rerun of *Die Hard*, others snuggled under festive fleece blankets.

As Anna scuffed into the room with yet more hot chocolate and cookies, she was surprised to hear the doorbell ring. Setting her treasures on the coffee table, giving Andrew a high dosage of stink eye when he reached for her snack, Anna slid across the hardwood floor, intentionally annoying him with the noise of her leather-bottomed slippers.

Still watching him, she pulled open the door with gusto, causing her flannel robe to expose her outfit of dancing reindeer and a blinking necklace from her dad.

"Eek." Hastily she closed the door while gathering the belt for her cover up. Once she'd run a hand over her head, hoping none of it looked as bad as it usually did, she opened the door a second time.

"Clare. Julian. What a surprise."

"Merry Christmas!" Clare shouted as she propelled herself into Anna's rib cage.

"I hope we're not interrupting anything." Julian looked sheepish as his eyes cast down toward his daughter. "Clare wanted to give you this." He handed a present to Anna.

"I'm sorry, come on in. We're just sitting around, eating too many cookies from Mari's mom."

Seconds later, the whole crowd of Millers had surrounded the surprise company. *It must be my new aura or something. Nobody ever showed up unannounced at my house in Albany.*

"Hi, Thomas family. It's nice to see you again." Julian and Andrew shook hands while her dad nodded a greeting from behind the crowd.

"Open my present. I made it for you." Clare pulled on Anna's sleeve, threatening to untangle the entire outfit again.

"Okay, but can we get coffee first?" Anna looked up at Julian. "Do you have time?"

"Thanks. That would be nice."

Andrew immediately took over for her. "I'll get the joe. Everybody, have a seat at the table."

"Thanks, big brother." Feeling silly as she shuffled in the noisy wool-and-leather slippers, she took a seat at the dining room table, encouraging Clare to sit next to her but the exuberant girl insisted on standing by her side, filling the gap between teacher and father.

Anna turned the gift over, running her finger under the taped edge of the angel-adorned paper. Preparing herself for a decoupaged frame, or worse. Anna gasped as she turned the gift over. Looking back at her was a sketch of herself teaching in the BarrSoren Academy lab. She was pretty sure Clare had chosen the first night of the survival class to memorialize.

As Anna ran her fingers over the glass protecting the exquisite pencil drawing, tears filled her eyes. Never, in her nearly thirty years of teaching, had a student honored her in such fashion. As the first tear started to fall, Anna tried to hide it with the back of her hand, but Clare was watching her so closely that there was no escaping her dismay.

"What's the matter? Don't you like it?" Clare leaned back into her father's arms, seemingly devastated by Anna's reaction.

As she looked at the girl's ashen face trying not to release her injured tears, Anna wanted to rip her own heart out. *How could I be such an ogre?* "Oh no, Clare, it's beautiful. I can't believe this."

"Then why are you crying?"

Julian gave her shoulders a gentle squeeze. "Sweetie, maybe Ms. Miller is just surprised."

Anna stared into his deep sable eyes, his worry about Clare reflected there. She placed the gift on the table and turned to hug the young artist. "Clare, this is the most beautiful gift I have ever received. I'm crying because I'm so happy to receive it. You're a very talented artist."

When she'd composed herself, Clare leaned back from her teacher. "It's the night we started planting the gardens."

"I know, sweetheart. And you did a great job capturing how much fun we had."

As she reined in her emotions, Anna's family passed

the picture around the table, each of them taken aback at the likeness of her.

Andrew came from the kitchen carrying a painted wooden serving tray with a giant carafe of coffee, cups, sugar, cream, spoons, and more butter cookies.

Anna groaned internally at how much weight she was probably gaining but everyone dug into the treat.

Julian stood from the comfortable gathering when the sun started to set on the western skyline. "Thank you for everything, but we should leave." He tousled Clare's hair as she reached for her coat. "This one has barn time tomorrow and I want to work on a special project while she's doing that."

"Dane didn't give you the time off?" The unfiltered question popped out immediately, putting Julian in the position of discussing personal information in front of her family.

Julian chuckled as he slid his arm into the sleeve of his coat. "Yes, actually, he did. But I've had a few ideas rattling around in here," Julian tapped his temple lightly, "that I need to commit to written word. And tomorrow's a perfect day for it. With Clare busy at the barn and everyone else out of the office, I can hammer away at the keyboard like a mad scientist."

As Anna walked them to the front of the house, her family belted out a string of Merry Christmases before drifting to the living room, instantly lowering themselves into the soft furniture and resuming the Bruce Willis movie.

Before she pulled the door open, Anna wrapped

Clare in a hug, kissing the top of the little girl's head. "Thank you again for a very special gift. I will hang it on my wall forever." The girl stepped behind her dad, her cheeks blushing.

And, without thinking, Anna stood on her tippy toes, wrapping her arms around his neck and kissed Julian on the lips. As he settled from the surprise, his arms enclosed her in his quiet strength, his mouth responding to her own.

When the kiss was over, she softly touched his cheek. "Merry Christmas, Julian."

JUST AS JULIAN stepped out his front door to take Clare to deliver her gift, he saw Jessica waving at them.

"Merry Christmas, neighbors." Handing a candy cane to Clare, the effervescent woman smiled at his daughter. "Did Santa bring you everything you wanted?"

Clare rolled her eyes but played along. "Absolutely. I wish I could thank him."

Jessica tipped her head and grinned. "Don't worry, I'll let him know."

Casting a suspicious glance at him, his daughter continued on to the Jeep.

"Julian, you're going to see Anna, correct?"

Now it was his turn to look at the cheerful woman curiously. "Yes. How did you know?"

"Don't worry about that, I know everything. Now I just wanted to tell you that there's still time—the magic is still there." She gave him a serious nod of her head. "And she's going to come to her senses. Just you wait and see. Now I'm off. Merry Christmas again."

For the life of him he couldn't figure that woman out. Everybody in town loved her. Personally, he wondered if she had a serious drinking problem. That would explain why she carried peppermints, and her cheeks constantly looked like someone had painted them a deep pink. He pushed the weird interaction to the back of his mind, climbed into his car, and took Clare the few blocks to Anna's house.

As they pulled up to her driveway, he was pleased to see her Sunburst parked in front of the garage with a heavy black charging cable running into the building. He wondered how many more times she'd have trouble with it in the New England weather. Even though Dickens was on the same parallel as Albany, the wind off the ocean made it much frostier. And the deep cold tended to play havoc with the batteries in an EV.

Anna answered the door wrapped in an open, faded flannel robe and Christmas pajamas, immediately gasping at the sight of them standing there. He thought she looked cute in the outfit. When she closed the door for a moment, he wondered whether she had been embarrassed for being seen by a parent and student wearing her jammies on Christmas afternoon. But when she reopened the door with the belt tied on her robe, she graciously invited them in.

Julian was a little surprised to find himself surrounded by several extra family members than he expected. But everyone was chill; the coffee and cookies were a perfect afternoon snack, and Anna loved the picture Clare had sketched of her. Honestly, he wasn't sure he could have asked for a better impromptu visit.

And then his world exploded, right after it tipped off its axis. He was fully unprepared for their exit to be so monumental. After hugging his daughter, Anna wrapped her arms around his neck, pulling him into a deliriously intense kiss. Even though he was aware of Clare tapping him on the back, he couldn't let go of Anna. He wouldn't let go of Anna. He wanted the kiss to go on forever.

But as the saying goes, all good things must come to an end. Well, they could always have continued the lip lock until one of them passed out from oxygen deficiency, but that didn't seem very sensible.

The more he thought about it, the entire kiss wasn't sensible. What was she trying to do to him? After she closed the door, he had to survive walking to the car with his young daughter while he had a raging erection.

The next morning, Julian dropped Clare at the Smith's house since all three kids were spending the day with Mari and her daughter, Penelope. Sitting in his office, his thoughts kept wandering back to Anna. "What am I supposed to do now? Was she high on holiday sugar treats or does she really want me?" Dating beautiful women had never been his superpower, and he'd already blown it once with this particular lady.

Staring at the football field-sized computer monitor,

Julian tried to recapture his thoughts from the night he drove her home from Creekside Academy. In the moment, he'd been in such a state of delirium to be sitting so close to her, that he hadn't fully memorized all his thoughts about the code.

As the flashing cursor taunted him, Julian wondered what had happened to his concentration. He loved writing code. *Why am I struggling here?*

Moments later, he heard footsteps in the anteroom of the suite he shared with Dane, then two knuckle wraps on the door. "Do you have a minute?"

Julian nearly tipped over backward in his chair at the sound of Anna's voice. Bolting to his feet, the motion shot his seat backward and it bounced off the wall behind him.

"Uh, yeah. Um, I mean, this is a surprise. I thought you were off until sometime in January."

"Well, somebody told me they would be working instead of returning presents to the store. And there was something I wanted to tell them."

Julian blinked a few times, wondering why she was referring to him in the third person. In mere seconds, he watched her hand flutter on one side of her head, tucking the same loose hair behind her ear. *She's nervous too.*

He extended his hand, leading her to sit with him on the generous leather sofa. "What did you want to say?" Julian tried not to smile when she moved closer to him, her jeans-clad thigh warming up his own. He couldn't believe how good it felt to have her so close to him.

Then she rose up on one knee, sliding her arm around his neck for the second time in as many days. Her lips grazed his mouth, reigniting yesterday's fire throughout his body.

Just when he thought his gonads would burst into flames, Anna pulled away from him, sucking on the tip of her tongue as she slid back on the couch, still driving him crazy without touching him.

After a few seconds she looked up at him again, this time with her tongue safely tucked inside. "I wanted to tell you that yesterday's kiss," her hand fluttered between them, "and this one, were real. I'm not joking, not playing you, and not interested in hurting you."

Julian cupped her face in his hands, peppering her cheeks and eyes with light nibbles and smoochy kisses. "Good. 'Cause I'm not, either. But you have to know something. I'm not very good at the whole dating thing."

She leaned into the leather, holding her belly as she laughed. "O.M.G. Neither am I. But there's something else."

Julian took her hands in his own. "You sound serious. Do I have to sign a prenup or something?"

After she chuckled at his idiotic question she took a deep breath. "It's about Clare. I won't hurt her fragile heart. We can only date if this is for real."

As Julian stared into her rich chocolate brown eyes, overwhelming emotion pushed him further into the deep end of the proverbial swimming pool. *How did I get so fortunate as to meet this beautiful woman who is putting my daughter's happiness ahead of her own?*

Standing from the sofa, Julian pulled Anna with him. "Let me tell you something, Ms. Miller. This is one hundred percent legit. I love you, Anna." Julian leaned his head down to her lips as she answered him.

"I love you, Julian. For real."

As she leaned against his chest, Julian's arms happily found their home wrapped around her.

THE END

THANK you for reading Wrapping Up Christmas.

Check out the next Dickens Holiday Romance, Call Me Crazy by Kathryn Hills.

In Dickens, the magic of Christmas might sneak up on you. In the snow and with a net. But true love always finds a way.

The prospect of a giant reset button is what brings business mogul Trevor Branstone to Dickens for Christmas. He's looking to shake off the breakup that's left him questioning his life choices. Renting a mountainside luxury home to relax and ski is exactly what he wants. And Trevor always gets what he wants. Quiet time alone will allow him to search his weary heart and brilliant mind for answers to the question... *What's next?* That is until he collides with a force known to townsfolk as "Becca." He's been warned: *"If she shows up on your doorstep with a passel of possums, don't let her in!"*

Rebecca Gallagher is searching, too ... under porches and behind dumpsters for the area's missing, injured, and abandoned animals. She's the Dickens Animal Control Officer, working tirelessly to help both domesticated animals and wildlife. Becca doesn't have a hot minute to question her mission. It's a calling—a life's purpose—and she takes names whenever someone or something gets in the way of saving a life.

Is there anything left over for her when the work gets done? And why is she so attracted to a man who might as well be from another planet? Then again... Skippy, her trickiest rescue yet, loves the handsome visitor, and that's saying something. Isn't it?

AFTERWORD

Dear reader –

I hope you've enjoyed my third book set in the fictional New England town of Dickens. If you haven't already read them, please enjoy more time in this magical place with Racing Through the Snow: The Christmas Derby and A Very Merry Monday.

It is no secret that I am an Indie author. Translation: I am my own publishing 'company.' With the help of a fabulous editor, Purple Pen Wordsmithing, LLC and the artistic talents of Kristian Norris, I do my best to offer readers professional work. If you find a mistake, please let me know at Contact - Gracie Guy.

If you haven't already, please check out my other books: The Secrets of Banyan Tree Bay Series, The New York Journey Series, the Passion novellas (all of which were inspired by trips that my husband and I took) and my other Christmas novellas.

Thank you for your support and happy reading –
    Gracie

ACKNOWLEDGMENTS

To my friend and ever creative assistant, LA, thank you seems so inadequate. Please know how much I appreciate everything you contribute to helping me navigate this career.

To my editor, Wendee Mullikin, your knowledge and tutoring always improve my writing skills. I love working with you.

To the children in my family – all thirty-two of you bring great joy to my holidays.

To my siblings and their families, I love you all beyond words!

ABOUT GRACIE GUY

Gracie Guy has been blessed with an eclectic and rewarding life, filled with family, friends and a passel of animals. She's a wife, sister, aunt, farmer, gardener, and retired athlete who loves her bionic hip. Gracie proudly calls Upstate New York her home.

Visit her website and All Author page as well as her Linktree.

ALSO BY GRACIE GUY

<u>**The New York Journey Series**</u>

A Fragmented Journey

The Journey Creekside

An Officer's Journey

A Cowboy's Journey

The Journey Home

<u>**Passion Novellas**</u>

Her Irish Passion

Her Carolina Passion

His Highland Passion

<u>**The Secrets of Banyan Tree Bay Series**</u>

What the Ocean Reveals

Beneath the Rubble (late 2024)

A Holiday Trilogy

Racing Through the Snow: The Christmas Derby

A Very Merry Monday

Wrapping Up Christmas: Moving on to a New Year

www.ingramcontent.com/pod-product-compliance
Lightning Source LLC
Chambersburg PA
CBHW022130170626
46808CB00002B/920